THE
DOUBLE-DIGIT
CLUB

THE DOUBLE-DIGIT CLUB

by

MARION DANE BAUER

SCHOLASTIC INC.

New York Toronto London Auckland Sydney
Mexico City New Delhi Hong Kong Buenos Aires

ISBN 0-439-70981-4

Copyright © 2004 by Marion Dane Bauer.
All rights reserved. Published by Scholastic Inc., 557 Broadway, New York, NY 10012, by arrangement with Holiday House, Inc. SCHOLASTIC and associated logos are trademarks and/or registered trademarks of Scholastic Inc.

12 11 10 9 8 7 6 5 4 3 2   5 6 7 8 9/0

Printed in the U.S.A.   40

First Scholastic printing, September 2004

For Myra Bauler,
who sees with her heart

CONTENTS

THE
DOUBLE-DIGIT
CLUB

CHAPTER I

MY LAST, MY BEST, MY ONLY

School was out. Fourth grade was done forever. And golden summer lay spread all around like butter melting into warm toast. Sarah paused in the middle of her front porch to breathe the lilac-scented air, then she tucked the doll she'd brought down from her room under her arm and headed across the lawn. What could be better than this? Her best friend, Paige, waited for her in their favorite play spot at the base of the line of lilac bushes that edged the yard.

"I brought Anastasia," Sarah announced, ducking into the leafy cave with the yellow-haired doll held out before her. "She'll be perfect."

"Perfect for what?" Paige asked, the dimples twinkling in her round cheeks.

I

"Perfect for practicing. Tomorrow's your birthday, you know."

"Oh." The dimples faded. "But we don't really need to practice again, do we?"

Sarah sighed, but she answered patiently. "Of course we need to practice. You know we do. This is important."

Paige ducked her head over her own doll, smoothing her dress and fluffing her coppery hair. It was a new doll sent by her grandmother for her birthday, and Paige's mother had let her have it a day early. "Maybe," Paige said, not looking at Sarah, "maybe she won't even ask me."

"You know Valerie Miller will ask you." Sarah sat down cross-legged on the packed dirt and pushed aside a bloom that drooped in her face. "You'll be ten. That's when she invites everybody—well, almost everybody—to join the Double-Digit Club."

"She didn't invite the Gomez twins," Paige reminded her.

"Well, no," Sarah conceded. "But they moved to Crystal Lake in the middle of the school year, and nobody knew when they turned ten."

The canning factory at the edge of their small Minnesota town sometimes attracted workers from Mexico, but at school the Latino kids kept pretty much to themselves. Juanita and Estelle were no different. Maybe they didn't even know about Valerie's silly Double-Digit Club. If they did, they were probably too smart to *want* to join.

"So," Paige said, the dimples appearing again, "when your birthday comes, she'll ask *you*."

Sarah shook her head. "But my birthday's not until the end of summer. Besides, she won't ask me. Valerie hates me."

"Valerie doesn't hate you." Paige sounded shocked. But then the idea of two people not liking each other always shocked Paige.

"Well, she doesn't like me. And I don't like her, either. But she'll invite you because everybody likes you."

Paige shrugged and said no more. Sarah looked away, out over the sun-splashed grass. The least Paige could do would be to argue a little more, insist that everyone liked Sarah too, no matter what she said.

"We've always agreed," Sarah reminded her. "It doesn't matter if we get asked or not. We aren't going to join the DDCs. Neither one of us."

"Of course we're not," Paige said at last.

Sarah relaxed then, at least a bit. She dug into her pocket for one of the caramels she'd picked up on her way through the living room and handed it to Paige. Paige smiled her thanks.

"Don't you miss playing with Kate sometimes?" Paige asked around the mouthful of candy.

"Yeah," Sarah admitted. Kate had been her

second-best friend, after Paige. The three of them had worked on their badges for Girl Scouts together, gathering leaves and pasting them up in a scrapbook and identifying them for their science badges. They had put on a play, too—Sarah had been the author—for their badges in arts and crafts. "And I miss Rachel and Therese, too. But they didn't have to go over to the DDCs. Nobody made them."

Once a girl was invited to be in Valerie's club she wasn't allowed to have anything to do with anyone who was still nine. The DDCs even quit going to Girl Scouts, which met after school the second Thursday of every month. They said being a Scout was "babyish," and by spring there were so few girls still attending that Mrs. Holmgren had given up and shut the troop down with no promises about when it might start up again.

Paige had cried each time one of their friends had turned ten and gone over to Valerie. Sarah had been sorry, of course, but she'd never cried. She refused to let Valerie Miller make her cry. And besides, she still had Paige, didn't she? Sarah and Paige had been friends since they were tiny, little kids, and Sarah didn't really need anyone else.

"It's a dumb club," Sarah muttered.

"Yeah," Paige agreed. "Who ever heard of starting a club with just one member?"

Sarah and Paige had laughed last fall when Valerie had come to school on her birthday and announced her new club. She was the only ten-year-old girl in the fourth grade, so, of course, she was the only member of the DDCs. But then the next week Renée Lukens had turned ten. And a few days later Paulette Schwandt had, too. Together they were the three most popular girls in the fourth grade. They'd practically run the Girl Scouts, and the Sunday School class at the Lutheran church most folks in town went to, as well.

Once those three were banded together into a club, every girl in their class started counting the days until her next birthday. Except for Sarah and Paige.

It wasn't just that they were the only fourth-grade girls with summer birthdays, either. They had decided right from the beginning that they wouldn't join Valerie's silly club no matter when they turned ten.

How often Sarah had wished, though, that her birthday were the one to fall on the first day of summer vacation, that Paige had to wait until August to be asked. It would have been fun to be the first girl ever to tell Valerie that she wouldn't join her stupid club. Still, she would be there to see Valerie's face when Paige refused her, and that was almost as good.

Sarah took the new doll from Paige's hands and looked it over. "I can see why your grandmother picked this one. She looks just like you." And she did: curls the color of a new penny, bright blue eyes. The doll was even a bit plump. Only Paige's freckles were missing.

Paige hated her freckles, but Sarah had always envied Paige the rich cinnamony spots that sprinkled her arms, her face . . . even her earlobes. Sarah's pale skin was boring in contrast.

"What are you going to name her?" she asked, fluffing the doll's hair.

Paige hesitated. "Well . . . I was thinking maybe . . . Gertrude?" The name came out sounding like a question.

"Gertrude?" Sarah tossed her head back and laughed. "You can't call a pretty doll like this Gertrude."

Paige flushed slightly, the color filling in the space between her freckles. "What would you name her?"

Sarah closed her eyes. This was something she was good at. Much better than Paige. She didn't know where the names came from, but when she saw a new doll or a kitten or anything at all that required naming, all she had to do was wait—for no more than a few seconds—and a perfect name always came to her.

"Gwendolyn," she announced, triumphant, handing the doll back. "Her name is Gwendolyn."

"Oh," Paige breathed. "That's pretty. And we can call her Gwen."

"Sure," Sarah agreed.

Paige took out the notepad and the stub of pencil she always carried with her and wrote it down. GWENDOLYN. "A scientist has to be ready to make notes on all important observations," she said.

"Especially the names of dolls," Sarah teased, and Paige giggled.

Paige was no more a scientist than Sarah was a queen, but still, she did well in math and science—the subjects Sarah wasn't so fond of—so maybe she would actually be a scientist one day. Maybe she would even be a scientist who made important observations about dolls. Paige loved dolls more than anyone Sarah knew. Most of the just-out-of-fourth-grade girls they knew thought dolls were babyish, and Sarah wasn't all that crazy about them herself—at least not anymore—but she enjoyed making up the stories she and Paige acted out with dolls.

Paige pocketed pad and pencil again.

"Now let's practice," Sarah said. "My doll—" She held up the one she'd brought from her room. Anastasia had long, straight, champagne blond hair and a tight little smile. "My doll can be

Valerie. Doesn't she look like Valerie? And Gwen can be you."

Paige held up her new doll. "And I go to the beach to celebrate my birthday. With you, of course. We should have brought another doll to be you. It's the beginning of summer vacation, just the second day, and I go to the beach and—"

"And Valerie comes up and says . . ." Sarah walked the Valerie doll up to the Gwen/Paige doll and said, in a high, artificially sweet voice, "Paige. How utterly *fantastic* it is to see you!"

"And Valerie will have all these girls with her, too. A whole clump of them. We should have brought lots more dolls."

"How fantastic to see you," Sarah repeated, lowering the Valerie doll's bent arm so that her hand rested on her hip in a snooty kind of way. "Today's your birthday, isn't it? Aren't you ten at last?"

"Yep," the Paige doll said. "Ten whole years. Which makes me as good as you, Valerie Miller. Doesn't it now?"

"That's great." Sarah nodded her approval. "Just right!" And then she continued speaking for the Valerie doll in a syrupy voice. "Of course you're as good as me, Paige Picotte. That's why I'm inviting you to be a DDC! You are going to join us now, aren't you?"

"Join you?" the Paige doll said. "You mean you want me to join your club?" The doll's hands flew up in the air, and the voice Paige used sounded properly horrified at the suggestion.

"Yes," the Valerie doll simpered. "I've been waiting all year for you to be ten so I could invite you. And today's your birthday. So what do you say?"

There was only one answer, of course. Paige would never leave her best friend alone and go off to be with those stuck-up prigs for the entire summer. But each time they came to this point in their practice, Sarah found herself holding her breath.

Paige walked her doll right up close to the Valerie doll, the auburn hair bright against the Valerie doll's pale, nondescript stuff, and when the two small faces were almost touching, she said, her voice filled with glee, "Why, Valerie Miller, I can't think of anything I'd like more than to be a DDC with you!"

Sarah was so shocked, she let go of her doll. Anastasia/Valerie toppled over like a miniature tree, burying her smile in the packed dirt beneath the bushes. Paige had toppled over, too. The girl, not the doll. She lay on her back, holding her doll in the air and giggling.

"Oh." She gasped. "Oh . . . you should have seen your face. You looked so funny!" Then she laughed and laughed.

Sarah pressed her lips together. How could Paige think that was funny? She reached up and stripped a lilac blossom from the bush, then sat examining the handful of confetti-like flowers that clung to her palm. She waited for Paige to be through with her silliness. "Come on," she said when the giggles had finally subsided. "Say it right. Tell me what you're going to say to Valerie tomorrow."

Paige sat up, suddenly solemn. "I'll say what you told me to," she said. And she let the words slide out in a solid stream. "'No-I-don't-want-to-be-in-your-club-Valerie-Miller-because-I-won't-go-anywhere-my-best-friend-Sarah-Raines-isn't-invited.'" She took a breath again and looked directly into Sarah's eyes. "Now . . . can we play something else?"

They were the right words, of course. In fact, they were exactly the words Sarah had made up for Paige to say. But there was something about the way she had said them, combined with "what you told me to," that spoiled them entirely. Still, there was a look in Paige's eye that warned Sarah not to suggest that she do it again.

"Okay," Sarah said, keeping her voice carefully neutral. She brushed her palms together to get rid of the ruined petals clinging to her hands. "What else do you want to play?"

Paige plucked a lilac blossom, too, but she twisted it off the stem whole and tucked it behind one ear. Then she crawled out from their cave, stood and began to spin in the midst of the green-blue day. "I want to play summer," she cried. "I want to play free. I want to play no school and no homework and no piano lessons and no . . . no anybody telling me what to do forever and ever and ever!"

And she spun and spun, holding her new doll in one hand. She whirled until her bright hair and the doll's bright hair seemed to blur, until the lilac blossom came flying out from behind her ear and landed in the grass.

Sarah smiled. She couldn't help it. It was what she wanted, too. Exactly. To play summer with Paige, to play summer and be Paige's friend— forever. So why was she worrying?

Sarah crawled out from beneath the sheltering bush, stood and began twirling, too. She started a new chant. "My last, my best, my only friend," she sang.

And as Sarah had known she would, Paige joined her. "My last, my best, my only friend."

They twirled and twirled and twirled—"My last, my best, my only"—until they collapsed side by side on the grass in a rush of new giggles.

CHAPTER 2

SAY IT!

Sarah could smell the lake before she and Paige were close enough to catch the first glimpse of the beach. Wet sand, lake weed, a touch of dead fish all mixed up together. Rich and dark, fresh and light at the same time. She and Paige had grown up with that smell. When they were babies, their mothers used to bring them to the beach and sit them at the edge of the water where the sand was hard packed and cool and the lake could lap at their toes. Maybe that's why they had always gotten along so well together, because they both loved the lake. Their very best times had always been spent here, taking swimming lessons, building sand castles, playing volleyball, even skating in the winter.

And early June was the best time for the beach. The sun blazed in a sky as blue as a robin's egg, and there was just enough breeze to take the edge off the gathering heat. Besides that, summer had barely begun. The summer people, the ones who had vacation homes here at Crystal Lake, a whole different house just to use for summer, hadn't started to move back in yet, so Sarah and Paige would have the beach pretty much to themselves. Except for a few mothers bringing their babies to sit at the edge of the water . . . and the DDCs, of course.

"Isn't it perfect?" Sarah exclaimed. "The whole summer is going to be just like this. I know it is."

A faint smile flickered across Paige's face, but was gone almost before it came. Paige was often quiet, but she had been especially so since Sarah had stopped by her house to pick her up. But then she was probably just nervous about talking to Valerie. She hated confrontation of any kind. Sarah knew that. Once the encounter with the DDCs was over, Paige would be back to her cheerful self again.

They turned into the Piggly Wiggly parking lot—a shortcut to the beach—but were no more than halfway across when Estelle Gomez zipped out from between two parked cars right in front of them, riding a skateboard. She whooshed across the smooth asphalt, stopping at the end of the lot where Juanita stood watching. Or maybe it was Juanita sailing across the pavement, her head up, her shining blue-black hair flying, and Estelle watching. Their teacher, Mrs. Wesley, had gotten so she could tell the twins apart, but as far as Sarah knew, no one else in their class had. The twin on the skateboard made a swift U-turn and stopped abruptly, the tip of the board in the air.

Paige applauded. The applause was the most enthusiastic thing Sarah had seen her do so far this morning. "You're really good," she called to the girl with the skateboard.

The twins turned to see who had spoken, surprise competing with the friendliness in their faces. When they saw Paige and Sarah, they nodded, but then they turned back to the skateboard without making any reply. The girl who had been riding it picked it up and spun the wheels, explaining something to the other.

Sarah and Paige moved on.

Sarah was sorry she hadn't called out to the twins, too. She had nothing against them. It was just that she'd never really gotten a chance to know them. Nobody had. During recess and lunchtime, the two always stayed off by themselves, talking to each other in a soft, musical Spanish, and to tell the truth, no one in their class had tried very hard to join in.

When Sarah stepped onto the beach, her sandaled feet sank into the tawny sand. The sunlight skittered across the surface of the lake, and she shielded her eyes with one hand to scan the area. She saw what she was looking for immediately. Across the way, in the dead center of the beach, the sunlight also reflected off a sheaf of blond hair displayed in pale perfection against an already brown back.

Valerie's family had gone to Florida for spring break, something no one else in their entire town had ever done as far as Sarah knew. And Valerie and her mother had both managed, somehow, to keep their early tans from fading. Maybe it was true that Valerie's mother actually allowed her to go to Pam's Tanning Parlor.

Six or seven girls were spread out around Valerie like spokes around the hub of a wheel.

"Let's stay here." Paige indicated the corner of the beach where they had stopped. "If we're close by the trees, we can have shade if it gets too hot."

"We don't want to stay here!" Sarah responded, surprised. But then, seeing the frown that creased Paige's face, she added, reasonably enough, "You know we've got to get this over with." She nodded toward the gaggle of girls. "We'll go over there and set up right next to them. Okay?"

"But—," Paige started to say.

Sarah didn't let her finish. She knew Paige. She would put any kind of unpleasantness off forever if she could. "It's your birthday," Sarah reminded her. "If anybody should have the middle of the beach, it's you."

Paige lowered her head and stood silently, drawing a semicircle in the sand with the toe of her sandal.

"Come on," Sarah said, and she began walking toward the girls, certain Paige would follow. When she was about twenty feet from the small group, she dropped her old striped towel onto the sand. The nearest girl stretched out on the sand was Kate Connolly. She looked up from her towel and half lifted a hand in greeting. Then she seemed to remember, and she turned her face away before Sarah could make any kind of a response.

When Sarah turned back to check Paige's progress, she was startled to see that her friend hadn't moved at all. She still stood in the corner of the beach by the trees.

Sarah dropped the rest of her load onto the towel: the beach bag holding the sunscreen her mother insisted she bring, her sunglasses, and two new paperback books. One for her and one for Paige. And the bag held a surprise, too: a package of Hostess chocolate cupcakes and ten candles.

Matches, too. She'd even remembered the matches. Paige loved Hostess chocolate cupcakes.

Sarah headed back to Paige. "What's the deal?" she asked, impatient now. "You aren't going to let them own the beach, are you? The way they owned everything at school? This beach belongs to us as much as to anybody. And the lake. The town, too."

"I just like it here," Paige replied, gesturing to indicate the shady patch where she remained rooted. "I don't want to get sunburned."

Sarah sighed. Paige did burn easily, but that had never kept her under the trees in the corner of the beach before. "Come on," she said, putting on the authority she sometimes had to use with Paige. "I've got plenty of sunscreen." And this time she put an arm around Paige's waist to make sure she came along. "Besides," she added, "you can't chicken out now."

"Why can't I?" Paige asked, and Sarah forced a laugh. Of course, she was joking!

A little kid, a toddler carrying a bucket and shovel, charged in front of them, heading for the water. His mother followed after, toting a baby on one hip, an oversized diaper bag pulling at her shoulder.

They should have brought buckets and shovels themselves. Making sand castles wasn't really baby stuff, was it? Though probably Valerie would say it was. Until the DDCs, Sarah had never had to ask such questions. She and her friends just did whatever they liked and whatever they liked was right for their age.

Valerie lay on an extravagantly large yellow towel in the center of the circle of girls. She sat up, smiling, as Sarah and Paige approached the spot Sarah had taken possession of a moment before. "Look who's coming!" she called to the other girls in a friendly voice.

Sarah hardly knew how to react. Was the game over? Maybe now that school was out, the DDCs didn't matter anymore. Maybe—

Then Renée sat up on her towel, too. "Hi, Paige!" she called. "Come on over. We thought you'd never get here."

So this was it! Sarah went hot, then cold, then hot again. She turned to face Paige. *Say it,* her eyes commanded. *Just like we agreed. Say it!*

But Paige wasn't looking at Sarah. She wasn't looking at the DDCs, either. She had gotten very busy laying out her towel, smoothing away a wrinkle, setting down her beach bag that contained the picnic lunch Paige had said she would bring.

There was a brittle silence, broken only by a teenage girl at the edge of the water. She was squealing while a teenage boy splashed her. She kept saying, "No, stop it!" but then she would splash him back.

Finally, Paige straightened. "Hi," she said. It wasn't an especially friendly hi, though it wasn't exactly unfriendly, either. More just flat . . . there.

Sarah looked from Paige to the girls, waiting.

"Happy birthday," Kate said. "I'm glad you're a double-digiter . . . at last."

Paige smiled shyly. She said nothing more, though it was clear everyone was waiting for her to speak.

"But she's not." The words burst out of Sarah's mouth. Had Paige forgotten what she was supposed to say? "I mean, just because she's ten doesn't make her part of your club."

She laid a hand on Paige's shoulder as she spoke, but Paige stepped away from Sarah's touch. Her face had gone pale. Even the freckles.

"We've got the cake." Valerie spoke directly to Paige, as though Sarah hadn't spoken, as though she weren't even there. She indicated a clear plastic cake safe at the edge of her towel, which Sarah hadn't noticed before. It held what looked like an angel food cake swirled with fluffy white frosting. Two fat pink candles, a one and a zero, spelled out the number *ten* on top. The sun's heat had drawn beads of moisture to the surface of the frosting, which gleamed like added decoration. "Then this afternoon we're going to the matinee, like I told you."

Like I told you. Sarah held her breath. Paige

hadn't said a word about talking to Valerie. But clearly Valerie had called her. Probably last night.

"My father's treat," Valerie added.

Valerie's father owned the movie theater in town—and just about everything else, too. At least that's what Sarah's father said. Sarah's parents were both teachers, and they didn't own anything except their house.

Sarah waited. *Say it!* she commanded Paige silently. *Tell them you don't even like angel food cake. Tell them your favorite is chocolate.* She wished now that she hadn't kept the Hostess cupcakes for a surprise.

But Paige seemed to be studying something in the sand next to her towel, and still she didn't respond.

Sarah closed her eyes. Paige wouldn't go over to the DDCs. She couldn't possibly.

"Paige, please," she pleaded at last in a low voice. "You've got to tell them."

Then Valerie, the princess herself, took over. "Come on, Paige," she said, rising from her yellow towel. Her voice was confident, bright. "I've left a place for your towel right here next to mine."

Sarah began to count silently. One . . . two . . . three . . . four. They would laugh about this later. Sarah would say, "The way you didn't answer at first, you had me scared. I thought you were actually going to do it."

Valerie had reached Paige. She was leaning over to pick up her towel, her beach bag.

"She's not coming," Sarah burst out, her voice too loud, too high. "She's not going to have anything to do with the DDCs. Isn't that right, Paige?"

Paige didn't answer. Neither yes nor no. She just stood there, her eyes darting from Valerie to Sarah and back to Valerie again.

"Paige!" Sarah knew she was yelling, but she couldn't help it.

Valerie crossed in front of Sarah, carrying Paige's towel and her beach bag back to her little circle.

And then Paige started to move. Her head low, she crossed in front of Sarah, too, following Valerie. She passed so close that the little hairs stood up on Sarah's arm as she went by.

For a moment Sarah couldn't breathe. It was as though the vivid blue sky had become a weight pressing down on her. Then finally, with the same deliberate care with which Paige had walked past, ignored her, Sarah picked up her towel and her beach bag and turned, plowing with labored steps back through the loose sand.

The girls' laughter trailed after her like poison gas. But she was not crying. She didn't think she would ever cry again. Not as long as she lived.

CHAPTER 3

WHO WANTS HER BACK?

"Sarah?"

Sarah looked up from her book. Her mother was standing in the doorway to her bedroom. A glance at the concerned expression she wore sent Sarah back to the book. Mom could see she was right here, sitting on her bed, reading *Anastasia Absolutely* for the fifteenth time. What more did she need to know?

"Look, Sarah." Her mother marched over to the bed, smoothed the rumpled covers, and sat down before proceeding with the speech she had clearly come to deliver. "You've hardly left your room for days. I know you're feeling bad, but don't you think—"

"I think all the time," Sarah said without raising

her eyes from the page, though she'd been reading the same two or three words over and over since her mother had come into the room. "I'll be spending the whole summer thinking. I don't have much else to do, do I?"

She knew she was being snotty, but she didn't care. The truth was she didn't care about anything anymore.

Her mother ran both hands through her short brown hair the way she did when she was exasperated. Sarah wished she would go away. She wanted her to stay. She didn't know what she wanted any longer.

Except maybe to strangle Paige. See her eyes bug out and—

"She'll be back, you know. You've been good friends for too long for a silly girls' club to separate you."

"Who wants her back?" Sarah muttered, her eyes still intent on the page where the letters seemed to be swimming under water.

Her mother didn't understand. No one who could call the DDCs a "silly girls' club" could possibly understand.

Not being ten yet wasn't a reason for keeping her out. It was an excuse. Maybe this had been Valerie's plan all along, to separate Sarah and Paige. To see Sarah without a friend left in the world.

Sarah had been right when she'd told Paige that Valerie didn't like her. And the truth was, she had never liked Valerie, either. Valerie was the kind of girl who'd been fussing with her hair and giggling about boys since the second grade. "Mature beyond her years," Sarah's mother might have said, and she would say the word *mature* as though it left a bad taste in her mouth. Sarah's opinion was that Valerie was just plain dumb. And Valerie thought Sarah . . . Well, of course, Sarah didn't know exactly what Valerie thought about her, but she was sure, given the way Valerie always made a point of ignoring her in school, that none of it was nice.

"Well," her mother said now, "I'm sorry about all this. I truly am. But I think it's time for you to do something. You can't spend the whole summer shut away in your bedroom."

"Do something?" Sarah looked up warily. "Like what?"

"I mean get outside, move around. Quit feeling sorry for yourself."

Quit feeling sorry for yourself! Sarah snorted. Was that what her mother thought she was doing?

"You know what the best remedy is for the blues?" Mom asked, putting on that too-cheerful tone she always used when she was about to dole out *important* motherly advice. "It's doing something for somebody who has more problems than you do."

Sarah started to snort again but thought better of it. Mom didn't have much patience for "attitude." So she asked instead, "Who has more problems than I do?"

"Lots of people in this world, sweetheart. Our next-door neighbor for one."

"Miss Berglund?" Sarah straightened up. "What's wrong with Miss B?"

Mom shrugged. "What do you think? She's old, she lives alone, she's blind."

"Is that all?" Sarah sank back against the headboard of her bed. She'd been afraid something bad had happened. Of course Miss Berglund was old. "Eighty-seven," she'd announce cheerfully whenever she got a chance. And of course she lived alone. She'd been living alone ever since her father, who'd long ago been pastor of the Lutheran church in town, had died. And that had happened before Sarah had even been born. And Miss Berglund had been blind for more years than Sarah had known her, too. One of Sarah's earliest memories was sitting very still so their neighbor could "see" her by running her cool, dry hands over Sarah's face.

Her mother drew back, her eyes striking a rather dangerous light. "Is that all? Isn't it enough?"

Sarah sat up straight, putting her book aside. If

she wasn't more careful about what she said, she'd end up in trouble with her mother for sure. She loved her mother. Of course. That's what you did with mothers, wasn't it? You loved them. But there was a place where she and her mother could never quite meet, and it showed most clearly in times like this, when Sarah was upset about something. Like the time that Sarah had wept over a small red squirrel with a white triangle on his chest killed on the road in front of their house. She had cried and cried over that squirrel until her mother had finally said, very firmly, "There are a lot of squirrels in the world, Sarah. You can't grieve over every one." Sarah had stopped crying, but that hadn't changed the way she felt.

"I didn't mean it like that," she said. "It's just that I don't think about Miss B's having *problems*. I think of her as Miss B, you know?"

Sarah's mother relaxed then. She smiled and reached to push Sarah's bangs out of her face. "That's because you're young."

"Yeah," Sarah answered grimly. "I'm young. Not even a double-digiter yet."

Her mother took Sarah's hand. "Those girls will get over it. I promise. Just give them time."

"How much time? The whole summer?" Sarah pulled her hand back. "And I don't care if *they* get over it or not. The only one of the whole bunch I care about is Paige."

"If you'd go to the beach," her mother pleaded, "if you'd just go to where they are, I'm sure—"

"No!" Sarah said it so fiercely that her mother stopped, mid-sentence, and didn't start up again. Were there no adults in the world who remembered what it was like to be a kid? Or had kids been different back then? Maybe they were always kind to one another when her mother was young. She didn't know.

Sarah put a slip of paper into her book as a marker and closed it. "I guess I'll go see Miss B," she said.

"Good. Good." A smile stretched her mother's face. And having accomplished her mission, she stood and headed for the door. "Tell her hello from me," she called back cheerfully.

"I'll tell her," Sarah replied, "that you said she has problems."

"Sarah Raines!" Her mother whirled around, hands on hips.

"You know I won't," Sarah conceded. But then, so as not to let Mom get the upper hand entirely, she added, "After I've visited Miss B awhile, I've got to come back to read my book. It's really good, you know."

What, after all, could her mother say about that? When school was in session, she was a reading specialist. Her whole job was to get kids to read!

Her mother sighed.

CHAPTER 4

EVERYBODY'S FAVORITE

"Hello, Miss B," Sarah called as she stepped through the front door.

She had an agreement with Miss Berglund. Sarah was to come on in without knocking—the door was never locked—but she was always to let Miss B know she was in the house. That way Miss Berglund didn't have to stop whatever she was doing to come to the door, but she wouldn't be startled by a sudden presence in the room with her. Nothing upset her more, she often said, than to discover someone nearby when she'd thought she was alone.

Sarah could hear Miss B's voice from the kitchen. "I know that's what you think," she was saying. "You've told me often enough. But it seems to me . . ." The fact that she was talking, however, didn't mean anyone was in there with her. Or that she was on the phone, either. Most likely, she was talking to "Papa," her dead father. She talked to him all the time. Often the conversations sounded a lot like arguments.

Sarah had once brought Kate to visit Miss Berglund. When Kate heard Miss B chatting away with her father, she couldn't decide whether to run out of the house terrified of Papa's ghost or to run out of the house terrified of the crazy lady. Sarah had never brought a friend here again. Except for Paige, of course. She and Paige knew that, while Miss Berglund might be what adults called "eccentric," she wasn't anywhere near crazy. As they had it figured, her papa probably hadn't given her enough chance to talk back when he was alive, so she was making up for it now.

Paige once said that the man in the portrait on the wall in the front room didn't look like anyone *she* would want to talk to, but maybe he was nicer than he looked. He was a minister, after all, and the ministers Sarah had known were all pretty nice. Scary sometimes when they stood up there in the pulpit in their black robes, but friendly enough when they stood at the front door after services, smiling and shaking hands.

Sarah moved past the portrait then through the dining room with its massive, old, lion-footed table.

"It wasn't like that at all," Miss B was saying from the kitchen just beyond.

"Hi, Miss B," Sarah called again from the kitchen doorway. "It's me."

"Oh, Sarah, hello!" Miss Berglund turned from scrubbing the sink to face the doorway where Sarah stood. Her lively smile always made Sarah forget the flat, impenetrable look of her eyes. She was wearing a bright purple pantsuit with a lavender blouse. Sarah and Paige often wondered how she managed, always, to match her clothes, but neither had ever seen her in anything that didn't go together.

Perhaps the ladies from the church who came every week to take Miss B shopping for groceries or to run other errands laid out her outfits for her, too. Though Sarah preferred to think that Miss B just knew, somehow, what color everything in her closet was, the way she seemed to know a lot of other things without being able to see them.

"Where's Paige?" Miss B added, as if to prove Sarah's thoughts about her.

"Don't know," Sarah replied.

"Oh? I thought you two girls were joined at the hip. Especially come summer."

"Well, we're not," Sarah snapped. She settled

into her usual place at the end of the kitchen table closest to the dining room door.

"Ah," Miss Berglund replied. Just that.

Sunlight splashed across the pale oak of the kitchen table, and Sarah spread out her hands to its glow. She wished Miss B hadn't mentioned Paige. Just hearing the name made her ache.

Miss Berglund got a tumbler down from the cupboard and a pitcher from the refrigerator and poured a glass of lemonade. She kept her hand wrapped around the top of the glass and stopped pouring just before it was filled. Sarah never had figured out how she managed that.

"Had a tiff, did you?" she asked, running her free hand along the edge of the table until she got to the end where Sarah sat, then setting the lemonade down in front of her. A plate of peanut butter cookies, golden brown and crisp looking, already sat in the middle of the table.

"No." Sarah took a sip of the lemonade. "We didn't have a *tiff*." The question made her instantly crabby. Maybe she should have stayed home with her book, despite her mother's badgering. Then she wouldn't have to talk about Paige. Still, when Miss B said nothing further, she felt compelled to explain. "She went over to the DDCs. That's all."

"Oh. The DDCs." Miss Berglund sat down with her own glass of fresh lemonade.

Sarah and Paige had told Miss B about the DDCs when the club was first formed, and she was one of the few adults who seemed to understand that the whole thing wasn't just some cute little children's game. "That's the entire purpose of some clubs," she had said, "to keep people out." Which was what Sarah thought, too. In fact, sometimes she wondered if the point wasn't to keep *her* out.

"What made Paige change her mind?" Miss Berglund asked now.

Sarah shrugged. "She didn't tell me. She just followed Valerie like a puppy on a leash."

"I'm sorry," Miss B said. And then she said no more. It was one of the things Sarah liked about Miss Berglund. She didn't pretend she could fix matters that couldn't be fixed, just because she was a grown-up. She didn't talk when there was nothing to say, either.

Sarah reached for a cookie—Miss B had always told her she didn't need to ask—and began to nibble mouselike around the edge, making the circle of cookie gradually smaller. She rummaged in her mind for another topic of conversation.

"I have an eye bouquet for you," she offered finally. Gathering eye bouquets was a game she and Paige played with Miss B. They would describe for her something they had seen recently, competing to come up with the most creative descriptions of ordinary sights. That way Miss Berglund said she could "see," too, in her mind's eye. Sarah was the one who had made up the game, and if she did say so herself, her descriptions were usually pretty good.

"I'm ready." Miss Berglund leaned forward from across the table, her face open and expectant.

But though Sarah had proposed the game, she didn't yet have anything to offer. All she could think to describe was the sun gleaming in Valerie's blond hair or the stubborn stiffness of Paige's back as she'd walked away, and she didn't want to say any of that. She glanced out the window toward the row of lilac bushes. "The lilac bushes are blooming," she began.

Miss B nodded. "When the breeze comes from the south, I can smell them. May was cool. The bushes bloomed late."

"And they're that shimmery color. Halfway between silver and purple. You know what I mean?"

Miss B folded her hands. "Shimmery. Halfway between silver and purple." She nodded. "That's it. That's it exactly."

A bit of warmth rose in Sarah as it always did when Miss B liked her descriptions. She went on. "The leaves are coming out now, too. And they're shaped like little hearts. Green hearts. The green of grass."

That wasn't very good. What could be more ordinary, more predictable than "the green of grass"? "The green of horses munching," she added, in a sudden flight of inspiration.

Miss B laughed and clapped her hands appreciatively. "Perfect!" she exclaimed. "Horses munching."

"Now I have one for you," Miss B announced. And she began to describe a black squirrel she'd "seen" run up a tree. Then the shape of the tree had turned into a black bear. Ever since Miss B had lost her sight, she had what she called visions. Leafy branches hanging in front of her that looked so real she'd reach up one hand to brush them aside. Faces. Most often "himself," which was the way she often referred to her father. When the visions had first begun, she'd been frightened and called her doctor. "No," he'd told her, "you're not crazy. It happens all the time when people lose their sight. I suppose it's just a bored brain amusing itself." So now she collected her visions and traded them with Sarah and Paige for eye bouquets. She didn't share them with anyone else, though. She said other folks might not understand.

Sarah leaned back in her chair. It was her turn again, but she was suddenly tired and out of ideas. The game wasn't so much fun without Paige here to appreciate her descriptions, too. "Oh, Miss B,

I wish . . ." She hardly knew what she wished. To have Paige back? Of course. But only if she came back in the right way. Properly sorry. Properly relieved to be out of Valerie Miller's clutches. The rest of the words tumbled out. "What will I do for a whole summer without her?"

Any other adult would have patted her on the head and told her that, of course, there would be lots of things to do this summer. And then they would have ticked them off: vacation Bible school at church, day camp at the city park, swim lessons at the beach—all the places Valerie was sure to be. Or, as her mother had been doing for the past three days, another adult might say that all she had to do was go where Valerie and her friends were and she was certain to be invited to join them. But Miss B didn't say any of that. She just sighed and said, "I know what you mean." Her sweet old face beneath her dandelion puff of white hair crinkled with sympathy. "When Papa was gone, I thought I couldn't live another day. I hardly knew how to get out of bed in the morning without him here, needing me."

The words brought a sting of tears to Sarah's eyes. She had known Miss B would understand. And comparing Paige's going over to the DDCs with a death wasn't an exaggeration, either. It was almost like a death. The death of their friendship.

Sarah gazed across the table fondly. Miss B sat

perfectly still, her hands folded on the table, apparently waiting for the next thing that would happen. Whatever that might be.

But Sarah didn't feel like waiting. She wanted the next thing to happen *now*. And she wanted the next thing to be Paige. She could see Paige in her own mind's eye, sitting quietly in the chair just around the corner of the table from where she was sitting, her coppery hair framing her face with soft curls. She would probably be holding Thomas Cat, Miss Berglund's big old black-and-white tom, stroking his thick coat and murmuring into his ear while Miss Berglund and Sarah talked all around her.

Miss B had been too wise to try to answer her question about how she would survive without Paige. So Sarah asked something she could answer. "Where's Thomas? I haven't seen him this morning."

"Probably asleep in the big leather chair in Papa's study," Miss B replied. "I was telling Papa just this morning, that old cat gets lazier every day."

"I'll go look for him." Sarah rose from the table. At least with Paige not here, she could have Thomas to herself for a change.

Maybe that's how she would get through the summer, by finding one thing after another that was better without Paige. Sarah almost laughed. Almost.

CHAPTER 5

COLLETTE

Thomas Cat wasn't asleep in the big leather chair in Papa's study. Sarah turned back, glanced through the living room and dining room—he wasn't curled up on a dining room chair or in his favorite place on the couch—then she paused at the foot of the stairs. For all the years she had visited Miss Berglund, she had never once been on the second floor. She knew she should ask before going up, but she didn't seem to have the energy it would take to walk back to the kitchen. Besides, Miss B was sure to say yes. Nonetheless, Sarah stayed to the edge of the steps as she climbed to keep them from squeaking. It would take only a moment to look on the second floor and be back down again.

The first room she came to at the top of the stairs must be Miss B's. A silver-backed brush and a comb lay side by side on the dressing table along with a few jars and bottles arranged in a straight line. And there was Thomas, curled on top of an elaborately crocheted bedspread. At Sarah's approach he opened one eye to a golden slit and greeted her with a chirping mew.

"Hello, Thomas." She ran a hand over his thick fur.

He yawned, his pink tongue curling behind his pointy teeth, and let his eyes drift closed again.

"Lazy old cat," Sarah scolded affectionately. But even as she spoke, her attention was caught by something beyond the cat. On a small, square table on the other side of the bed stood a glass dome, and enclosed inside the dome was a doll. About fourteen or fifteen inches tall. The most beautiful doll Sarah had ever seen.

Sarah walked around the bed to inspect the figure more closely. When she bent to peer through the glass, she could have sworn the doll smiled back at her. The tiny mouth, barely tipped at the corners, was so mischievous, the heavily lashed eyes so alive that she seemed ready to leap through the protective glass into Sarah's hands.

"Who are you?" Sarah whispered, but even as she asked, she already knew. This was Collette. She didn't know where the name came from. It was just there, waiting for her to say it out loud. So she did. "Collette." The name was perfect. And the sparkle in Collette's bright blue eyes seemed to indicate that she thought so, too.

Sarah knew she shouldn't touch anything in the bedroom. Her mother had often reminded her not to meddle with Miss B's belongings. That was especially important, Mom said, because Miss Berglund wouldn't be able to see her doing it. But the glass dome was in her hands being lifted away almost before she had time to think whether she should touch anything or not. She wasn't really meddling, though. She certainly wasn't moving anything or taking anything away. She was only going to stroke the rosy cheeks and touch the green taffeta dress.

"Paige would love you!" she told Collette.

"Mrrrr!" It was Thomas Cat registering a sharp objection to being ignored. Sarah had forgotten him so completely that she almost dropped the dome at the intrusion. Gasping, she steadied the delicate glass in her hands and replaced it gently over the wooden base. What a lot of explaining she would have had to do if she'd broken it! She took a deep, slow breath and stepped back from the table.

Collette's smile seemed to have grown more pale now that she was beneath the glass dome again. Why would anyone keep such a beautiful doll shut away like that? But then, she could hardly ask Miss B a question like that. She hadn't even told her she was coming up here.

Sarah scooped Thomas into her arms and headed quickly and quietly back downstairs. "I've got him," she told Miss B, who was back at the kitchen counter, forming bread dough into loaves. Sometimes she let Sarah and Paige make their own small loaves, but Sarah wasn't interested now. She had the cat.

Settling into her chair with Thomas in her lap, Sarah began to rub his head, exactly the way Paige always did. He didn't even purr, though, only waited for a few seconds then jumped down and stalked away, his tail twitching. So much for anything being better without Paige!

If a doll could choose, Collette would probably prefer Paige, too.

But Paige was a DDC now. She was too big and important to be bothered with dolls, no matter how fine.

Sarah picked up her glass of lemonade then put it down again without taking a swallow. If she didn't say Paige's name, she thought she might burst. "Paige loved dolls," she blurted out. She noticed, even as she said the words, that she was speaking of Paige in the past tense. Almost as though she had died.

"I loved dolls when I was a girl, too." Miss B

had formed a loaf from the dough, and she laid it in a waiting pan. "Or at least there was one doll I specially loved. I named her Nancy."

"Nancy?" Sarah couldn't help but be disappointed. The doll she had seen was no more a Nancy than she was Minnie Mouse.

"I have her still." Miss Berglund had grown pensive. "She's on the table next to my bed."

Sarah's heart began to thump. "Oh?" she said, as though she knew nothing about such a doll. She hoped she sounded more innocent than she felt.

"I was your age exactly when my mother gave her to me. I think Mama gave her to me then because she already knew she wasn't going to be with us much longer."

Miss B had told the story more than once. Not about the doll, but about her mother's dying when she was nine years old. A chill always passed through Sarah at the thought of a girl her own age being left without a mother, being left responsible for all the work of this big house.

"But the doll," Sarah said, leaping on the opportunity to find out more. "You still have her? She must be very old."

Miss B nodded. "Near a hundred years, I'd say. She'd been my mama's when she was a girl."

One hundred years old! Sarah couldn't think of anything else she knew that was that old. She wished even more now that she'd told Miss

Berglund she'd been upstairs, that she'd already seen her doll. Miss B wouldn't have minded. It seemed too late for that now, though, so she said only, "I'll bet she's beautiful."

"Oh," Miss Berglund said softly. "She is."

"Paige would have loved to see her." She seemed unable to quit talking about Paige, though the name caught in her throat every time she said it. It was true, though, Paige would have loved Nancy . . . Collette.

Sarah straightened, an idea gathering slowly. Maybe it was a kind of sign, going up to Miss B's bedroom for the first time ever and seeing the doll. Maybe there was a reason Miss B had kept Collette standing beneath that glass dome all these years.

That doll might be exactly what Sarah needed to bring Paige back.

CHAPTER 6

ONLY BORROWING

Several days later, Sarah was still thinking about Collette, about how delicately beautiful she was, how unexpected standing there next to Miss Berglund's bed, when she ran into Paige in the Piggly Wiggly. Literally. She bumped the grocery cart into the backside of a girl bending over the boxes of Froot Loops on a bottom shelf.

"Oh," Sarah said. "Oh. I'm sorry." And then, peering around the overflowing cart, she realized who the backside belonged to. Had Paige always been so chubby? And since when did she like Froot Loops? They had always agreed that Froot Loops tasted like stale jelly beans. Paige's favorite cereal, like Sarah's, was Wheat Chex. But maybe Paige wasn't loyal to cereals anymore, either.

Paige straightened slowly, looking first at Sarah then down at the back of her scuffed ankle, but she didn't speak, not even to acknowledge the apology. Then their two mothers started talking, right over their heads, and if they'd wanted to talk to each other, there was no way. Unless, of course, they'd moved off down the aisle a short distance as they would have done in the past.

But Paige gave no sign of wanting to move anywhere.

Sarah stood, as tongue-tied as if she'd bumped into some famous movie star, turning one opening after another over in her head and discarding them all. *How's Valerie?* sounded like an accusation. *Are you having a nice summer?* wasn't much better. And the thing she really wanted to say, *I've got something, something you'd love,* was a complete lie. She didn't *have* Collette. She hadn't even figured out how to get back upstairs in Miss Berglund's house to see her again.

If only she did have the doll, though. Paige would come to her house to see Collette in a minute.

Sarah wanted to explain how beautiful the doll was, how valuable, too. She wanted to tell Paige that she'd gone to the library and found a book on antique dolls and discovered that this one was made of an unglazed china called bisque. And that Miss B had said she was probably close to one hundred years old.

She also wanted to take Paige's arm and shake her, to tell her to quit acting so stuck up and so like a DDC.

But Paige seemed not to know she was in danger of being shaken. She picked up a Froot Loops box and began to read the print on the back, peering at it intently as though the list of vitamins and minerals, carbohydrates and fats and sugars were the most fascinating story on earth. Sarah backed the heavy cart away and maneuvered it on down the aisle. The last thing she heard was Mrs. Picotte saying to Paige, "Do you really want Froot Loops? I didn't think you liked that one."

Good, Sarah thought. I hope her mom buys it and makes her eat every stupid bite.

But then Sarah's own mother was beside her, whispering fiercely. "Why didn't you speak to her? Couldn't you see she was waiting?"

But Sarah couldn't see. All she had seen was Paige's back.

Her last, her best, her only friend.

Sarah went to visit Miss B every day, and at least that pleased her mother. She didn't go to the beach, though. And when it came time to sign up for vacation Bible school she said no, she didn't want to go this year. At first she thought her mother was going to make her, but then Mom sighed and said, "All right, Sarah. But I'm afraid it's going to be a long, lonely summer if you go on this way." Sarah figured it was going to be a long, lonely summer whatever way she went.

She didn't go to the movie theater, either. Not even when they were showing a new movie, the kind she liked that had a kid in it or maybe a dog. She told herself she could go to those places if she wanted to. She just didn't want to.

In the long, boring summer evenings, her dad took pity on her and started teaching her how to play chess. She wasn't very good at it—Dad always won, even though he tried real hard to help her and even showed her moves she'd over-looked—but anything was better than sitting in her room or out on the porch, slapping mosqui-toes. Her father was the math teacher at the high school—he taught summer school through the first months of summer—and he was real good at things like chess. If she'd been playing with her mother, she might have had a chance.

She walked to the library nearly every day, and though she'd run out of Anastasia books, she dis-covered that Lois Lowry had written lots of other good ones, too. *Autumn Street* had made her cry. And then there was *The Giver*. She wasn't sure she understood it all, but sometimes what a story made you feel was more important than under-standing every little bit.

Finally, the day came when she could stay away from the doll no longer. She simply had to see Collette again. Just to look at her. That was all she was going to do. Just look.

"Where's Thomas Cat?" she asked Miss B once more, looking up from the pile of strawberries she was hulling at the kitchen table. One for her mouth, one for Miss B's preserves. ("They're as red as a clown's nose," she had told her. Miss B had told about seeing her father's face floating against a backdrop of summer sky, like a cloud.)

"Thomas Cat?" Miss Berglund said, hesitating with the measuring cup still immersed in the sugar canister. "I'm pretty sure I let him out this morning."

She had let him out, Sarah knew. In fact, Sarah had seen him lying in the sun on the front porch when she'd arrived. "Maybe," she said, keeping her voice carefully casual, "he's in your father's study." It wasn't a lie. Only a maybe. She would never lie to Miss B.

"Maybe," Miss B said cheerfully. "Why don't you go look?"

Sarah was already standing up, rinsing the fragrant red juice from her hands. "I'll be right back," she said, making her voice cheerful, too.

She didn't even stop to peek into the study. There was no point. She headed, instead, for the stairs.

Once inside Miss Berglund's bedroom, Sarah let her glance skitter over all the surfaces as though she really did expect to see the black-and-white cat there, but even as she pretended to look, she made her way to the table on the opposite side of the bed.

"I'm not hurting anybody," she reassured herself as she lifted the glass dome away. "Especially not you," she reminded the exquisite doll. Why, Miss Berglund might even have loaned Collette to her if she'd asked. Only she seemed to have gotten herself into too much of a tangle to ask.

Sarah lifted the doll off the stand that supported her and held her out for closer examination. She looked under her dress and saw that the body was stuffed, made of pieces of white leather carefully stitched together. Her china face and arms and legs were flesh-colored and cool. Her chestnut-colored hair glowed, even in the half light of the curtained room, and her eyes were knowing, though exactly what they knew was hard to decide.

Sarah smoothed the taffeta dress, the vibrant green of emeralds. She had never seen emeralds, actually, but they could hardly be more beautiful than the lustrous green fabric.

"Your name is Collette," she whispered. "You are a model, a movie actress . . . no, a queen."

Collette's smile seemed to agree with every possibility.

If Paige could only see. Just once. She wouldn't be able to resist this doll. Not for an instant.

Sarah sighed and started to put Collette back. But even when she had the doll clasped in the stand that reached around her waist to hold her up, she couldn't make herself lower the stuffy glass dome to cover her. How unfair it was to leave such an exquisite doll standing here, day after day, with no one even to see her . . . let alone to take her out and play with her. If dolls could be lonely, Collette certainly must be.

Lonely exactly the way Sarah was.

Sarah loved Miss B, her parents, books, but she didn't think she could stand another day of hulling strawberries, playing chess, reading. Moreover, her mother was beginning to get on her case. She was saying things like, "This has gone on long enough. Why don't you call her . . . just once. You know Paige. She's always been a little shy. She's probably just waiting for you to break the ice."

But Sarah wasn't so sure. Was that what Paige was waiting for? And if she did call, what could she possibly say? "Hi! Long time, no see"?

If she had Collette, though, if she really had her, the call would be a cinch. "Guess what, Paige. I've got this doll. She's the most beautiful doll ever. Do you want to come see?"

Sarah stood looking down at the bisque face. It was perfect, without the tiniest flaw. Her palms were growing sweaty, and she wiped them, one at a time, on her shorts. Then without ever deciding it was what she was going to do, she lifted Collette, once more, from the stand, tucked her into the crook of her arm, and carefully replaced the glass dome.

When she reached the door of the bedroom she looked back. Miss B would never know. Nothing was out of place to the touch. Nothing. And the church ladies who came to help Miss B had been there yesterday and wouldn't be back until next week. Sarah would have Collette returned to her place under the dome long before that. Why, she would put her back tomorrow. All she needed was enough time to show her to Paige.

Sarah walked down the stairs, slowly, quietly—there was nothing wrong with Miss B's hearing—holding Collette against her beating heart. At the bottom of the steps she stopped. She couldn't go back into the kitchen carrying the doll. Even knowing that Miss B couldn't see, she couldn't do it. Collette would burn up in her hands if she tried.

So she moved instead to the front door and pulled it open.

"Sarah?" Miss B called from the kitchen. "Are you leaving so soon?"

"No, Miss B," Sarah called back. "I'm just checking outside. Thomas Cat wasn't in your papa's study. I thought maybe he's out here."

And as if the suggestion had brought him,

there was Thomas, stretched out on the cushions of the porch swing, his golden eyes half shut.

"I see him," Sarah called, forcing her voice to sound bright. "You were right. You did let him out this morning." Then she walked over to stroke his head and scratch the white patch along his jaw. Paige had always said it was his favorite place to be scratched, and she must be right. He stretched his neck and purred.

Sarah set Collette down gently in the corner of the swing. Thomas narrowed his golden eyes and quit purring. He sniffed the doll's foot.

"I'm only borrowing her," Sarah whispered fiercely. "I'm going to put her right back."

But when she went to pick Thomas up instead, he clearly had no intention of allowing himself to be carried into the house. He wiggled and squirmed, twisted in her arms. When an outstretched claw nicked her and she dropped him with a small cry, he landed on his feet and stalked away across the porch, his tail twitching in annoyance. Maybe he knew she didn't have permission to borrow the doll.

Sarah watched the cat disappear around the corner of the house, then turned back to Collette. She seated the doll more securely and smoothed her taffeta dress. "Don't worry," she promised. "Everything's going to be fine. Just fine."

But whether she was talking to the doll or to herself, she wasn't sure.

CHAPTER 7

JUST YOU WAIT

Sarah sat cross-legged in the middle of her bed, a portable telephone receiver in her hand, Collette perched on her pillow.

"Hi, Paige," she murmured, speaking not into the silent phone but to the mid-distance of her room, "you'll never guess what I've got."

She shook her head. If she'd called a week ago and said that, Paige would have come right over.

Sarah knew Paige well. She knew her so well, in fact, that she'd half worried about what would happen on Paige's birthday from the time Valerie Miller had formed the DDCs. She'd worried and told herself she had nothing to worry about and worried again. Paige always wanted everyone to like her, even people she didn't especially like herself. So though having her go over to the DDCs had been a terrible shock, it was not a surprise. The problem was that now she'd done it, Sarah seemed to have lost all ability to predict what Paige might do or say next.

Sarah gazed out the window toward the lilac bushes that separated her house from Miss Berglund's. Most of the blooms had faded to the pale, translucent amber of tea. They looked like old lace now. The next time she saw Miss B she needed to describe that for her.

She lifted the still-silent phone to her ear and tried again. "Hello. It's me. Your friend. Aren't you tired of those stuck-up girls in the DDCs yet?"

Did that seem like begging? Did she care? If Paige came back, what else mattered? Or maybe they could just start over, pretending nothing bad had ever happened. "Hey, Paige," she tried next. "Want to come over?"

Sarah sighed, punched the talk button on the phone and, when the dial tone hummed distantly, punched it off again. Nothing was right. Nothing! It was as though there were no right words left. For years she'd never had to think what to say to Paige when she picked up a phone or went to her front door or saw her at school. They just looked at each other or heard the other's voice and started talking. Now she'd give anything to be able to talk to Paige so easily again. Miss B always said that you should appreciate what you have when you have it. Sarah had never known how right she was before now.

Did Miss Berglund feel that way about her vision? She must. Who appreciates all the incredible sights a person's eyes take in every day of the world? Sarah's glance traveled around her room, pausing at the sprigs of yellow daisies in her wallpaper, at the ceramic frog, magnificent in his greenness, sitting on her dresser, at Collette reclining against her bed pillow with her pixie smile. "Just wait till Paige sees you," Sarah said, reaching out to touch the doll's cool cheek.

She'd managed that afternoon to sneak the doll into the house and up the stairs without anyone's seeing. Now her mother was getting groceries, so she and Collette had the house to themselves for a brief time. But as soon as Mom came back, the doll would have to be tucked away out of sight. Just in case one of her parents came into her room and started asking questions. All of which meant she didn't have time to play with Collette or even look at her very much. Only time to show her to Paige if Paige would come right over.

None of that mattered, though. Once Paige saw Collette, Sarah could hide the doll away until morning when she'd be able to put her back under the glass dome in Miss B's bedroom. She'd find some excuse to slip up there again. And then this whole thing would be over—except that Paige would be back. She would be impressed with how much Sarah was willing to go through for her best friend, and she would be back for good.

"So," she ordered herself, "do it!" And she closed her eyes and dialed. She'd been dialing Paige's number for almost as long as she could remember, and she didn't even need to look at the buttons on the receiver to get it right.

The rings sounded hollow, as though the phone at the other end were ringing in a cave.

"Hello?"

Sarah opened her mouth, ready for whatever was going to come tumbling out, but then she realized. This wasn't Paige. It was Paige's older sister, Darcy. "Hi," Sarah said. Suddenly she was out of breath. "Is Paige there?"

"Oh, hi, Sarah. Haven't seen you around here for a while. Have you been sick?"

"No," Sarah lied, because she had been, hadn't she? Sick at heart? "Just . . . just busy. My mom is making me help this blind old lady next door." Even as she said it, her cheeks burned. What was happening to her? She'd never referred to Miss Berglund as a blind old lady before.

"Bummer," Darcy said. "That's a real bummer. Just a minute. I'll get Paige."

While she waited for Paige to come to the phone—or not to come, who knew?—Sarah picked up Collette and put her in her lap . . . for luck. She crossed her fingers, too. All four fingers on both hands, then crossed her wrists and thumbs as well. Her ankles were already crossed.

"Hello?" Darcy must not have told Paige who was calling. She sounded friendly.

"Hi. It's me . . . Sarah." That was a dumb way to start. They knew each other's voices the way they knew each other's favorite foods and favorite movie stars and favorite . . . just about everything.

"I know," Paige said at the other end. And then, after another pause, "Hi."

"Do you want to come over? I've got a doll. She's really beautiful. I know you'd love her." The words came tumbling out. Was that what she'd meant to say?

Another pause, heavy with meaning Sarah couldn't interpret. But then the familiar voice came back. "Yeah. Sure! I really would . . . if . . . I mean, if it's okay."

"If it wasn't okay," Sarah replied, lowering her voice to cover the sudden hoarseness that seemed to have crawled into her throat, "I wouldn't have asked you . . . doofus." It was a word Sarah had learned from her grandfather, something she and Paige called each other when one of them was being silly.

Paige giggled. "You want me to come now? We've only got about an hour before supper."

"Yeah, come now. Maybe my mom will let you have supper here. At least you'll have time to see the doll."

"Okay. I'll—I'll be right over." And a loud click resonated in Sarah's ear.

After Sarah had turned off her own phone, she sat with the receiver in her hand. For a long moment she sat perfectly still, then slowly she lifted it to her mouth and kissed it.

Paige was through with the DDCs. She had to be. Maybe she hadn't liked being with them after all. Maybe she'd regretted going over the moment Sarah had walked away from the beach. Whatever. Life was good again. Very, very good.

Sarah picked up Collette and kissed her, too.

"Wait till Paige comes," she told the doll. "Just you wait. You're going to love her."

CHAPTER 8

MONKEY-SEE-
MONKEY-DO!

"She's the most beautiful doll I ever saw." Paige sat at the foot of Sarah's bed, holding Collette reverently. She smoothed the rich, auburn hair, lifted the dress to study the petticoat and the lace pantaloons underneath. "Where did you get her?"

Sarah told the tale eagerly. About going upstairs in Miss Berglund's house looking for Thomas Cat, about seeing the doll, about Miss B's saying her name was Nancy but that she had named the doll Collette.

"The moment I saw her, I knew that was her name," she said.

A cloud seemed to pass over Paige's face—Sarah didn't know why—and Sarah hastened to add, "I knew right off you would love her, too."

The cloud slipped away again. Paige ducked her head, a smile tugging at the corners of her mouth. Clearly, she was pleased that Sarah had been thinking about her.

So Sarah rushed on, explaining about the doll's being a gift from Miss B's mother when she was nine years old.

"Miss B must really love this doll," Paige said.

Sarah nodded, but her mouth was beginning to go dry. How could she tell Paige the rest? She hadn't mentioned that Miss B didn't even know she'd been upstairs. Or about going again secretly, pretending to look for Thomas. Or even worse, about the way she'd taken Collette out of Miss B's house without asking permission. She certainly couldn't say, now that the doll had worked her magic on Paige, that she had to hide her away as soon as her mother came home and then slip her back into Miss Berglund's house first thing in the morning. Why hadn't she thought about how hard the whole thing would be to explain? It was something she should have considered before.

If she made something up, Paige usually knew she was lying. The two of them had always been able to read each other's thoughts. Like the time Paige had watched a horror movie before Sarah had come for an overnight, and even though Sarah hadn't seen the video and Paige hadn't told her about it, Sarah was the one to have night-mares, complete with scenes from the movie.

"So Miss B gave her to you," Paige finished for her, her round face beaming.

"Yeah," Sarah agreed. "That's the way it was." She concentrated for a moment on scratching a mosquito bite on her knee. Then she added, "Collette isn't any use to her anymore—I mean since she can't see her and all—so she said I might as well have her. Actually, she said that *we* might as well have her. At least for a while. She knows how much you like to play with dolls."

Paige hugged the doll. "Oh, Sarah. Miss B is so nice. I'll go by and thank her on my way home."

"Oh! You don't need to do that!" The response leaped out of Sarah's mouth. "I mean . . . you know Miss B. She doesn't want to be thanked."

Paige gazed at her quizzically, her head tipped to one side. "Of course, she wants to be thanked. What do you mean?"

Sarah's brain was spinning. "Well . . . see . . ." She stumbled, stopped, tried again. "The way I told you . . . It wasn't quite like that." She was going to tell Paige the truth. She really was. But there was something, a look in Paige's eyes, that stopped her. Skeptical? Blaming? What right did this traitor, this member of the DDCs, have to blame her? For anything?

She took a deep breath. "I mean, Miss B didn't really give her to both of us. I just said that so you wouldn't feel bad. The truth is, she gave her to me."

"But she knew you'd share her with me." Paige's voice rose slightly. "She knows I'm the one who likes dolls, that you don't like them all that much. At least that's what you always say. So there's no harm in thanking her."

No harm in thanking her. Sarah ducked her head. She had to think fast. She started scratching the mosquito bite again, but then stopped. She put some spit on the tip of her finger and touched it to the now-raw bite to make it sting instead of itch. "Yeah," she said, keeping her eyes on her knee, "she knows you like dolls. But she knows how you went over, too. To the DDCs." The very air in the room seemed to have grown heavy. Sarah lifted her chin to look directly at Paige. "I guess she thought that was pretty mean, going off and leaving me alone like that."

"You told her?" Paige had gone pale. "Why did you go and tell her?"

Sarah shrugged. "Why not? It's not like it wasn't true."

"And so she . . . blames me?" Paige sounded short of breath.

"Well . . . she doesn't exactly blame you." What had Miss B said? Sarah couldn't remember.

"More, I guess, she was feeling kind of sorry for me. Being left alone like that."

Paige said nothing. She sat touching the doll, moving her limbs, tipping her back so that her eyes closed and then bringing her upright again.

Sarah hadn't meant to mention the DDCs at all. She'd been waiting for Paige to say something about the club. Now, since the topic was out in the open, she asked, "How do you like being one of *them*? Is it fun?" The question came out sounding sarcastic, which wasn't what she had intended, but she let the sarcasm lie there between them.

Paige shrugged. "Sure." But she didn't look at Sarah. "Why not?"

Why not?

"A little boring, maybe. But fun."

Sarah stared. *Boring but fun?* Was Paige serious?

"We do things like sit around and paint our fingernails, each nail in a different color. Then everyone votes on which color is right for you, and you take the polish off the other nine nails and do them all over in your color."

Sarah checked Paige's fingernails. They were painted a pale lavender. A rather dull color. Nothing anywhere near the shimmer of lilacs. Was that the color the DDCs thought was "right" for Paige?

"What if you don't agree with the vote? What if you like a different color than the one they choose?"

"No one disagrees." Paige shook her head emphatically. "That's the point of being in the DDCs. No one ever disagrees." She met Sarah's gaze for the first time.

"Do you *like* that?" Sarah couldn't imagine it. Why, Paige sometimes complained that *she*, Sarah, was bossy. If they ever had a fight it was over Paige's not wanting to do whatever it was Sarah had proposed.

Paige shrugged.

"Lemmings." Sarah shook her head. They'd read a story in school once about lemmings. They were little animals that would get to running, following one another. They would even follow the leader off a cliff, one after the other, and die.

And then Paige's grin broke through. "Lemmings," she agreed. "Monkey-see-monkey-do!"

"You mean . . . you mean . . ." Sarah couldn't believe it. "You mean you don't like being in the Double-Digit Club?"

Paige held the doll in front of her face, lifting one delicate arm as though Collette were about to speak. "I hate it," she said, in a light, breathy voice that seemed to pass through the small china face. "It's the dumbest thing I've ever done in my whole life. I hate being told what to do all the time."

Sarah whooped with laughter. She couldn't have dreamed a better answer! She leaped off the bed and spun in the middle of the room, wrapping her arms around herself to keep from flying into a million pieces with pure happiness.

"Then you're not going back!" she said when she could stop spinning.

"Not going back," Paige echoed, still in the breathy doll's voice.

"Ever!" Sarah cried.

"Ever!" Collette agreed.

"And so we're friends again!"

"My last, my best, my only friend," Collette recited.

Suddenly Sarah didn't want the doll between them. She wanted to hear Paige directly. She reached out to move Collette away from Paige's face. "You say it," she urged. "I want to hear it from you."

"Say what?" Paige looked confused, as though she had stepped out of the room and missed the last part of the conversation between Sarah and the doll.

"My last, my best . . . ," she prompted.

"My only friend." Paige filled in the last quickly, automatically.

It was not what Sarah wanted. Not exactly anyway. She wanted to hear the whole thing . . . in Paige's voice. She wanted to hear her say it as though she meant it. But she mustn't insist. Paige had said it, after all. Almost twice. And she had come back, too. Hadn't she?

"I missed you," Sarah said softly. "I really, really missed you."

Paige didn't say "I missed you, too," the way Sarah had expected. But she did look up and smile. "Let's play with Nancy," she said.

"Collette," Sarah corrected automatically.

Paige looked down at the doll and said nothing.

CHAPTER 9

IT'S NO WONDER

Sarah sat on the edge of the bed, studying Paige. She had changed. Something was different. For one thing, Paige had never argued about the names she chose. She'd always said she liked them before.

"I'm sure Miss B would like the name Collette." Sarah spoke slowly, distinctly, as though Paige might not understand otherwise. "Besides, it's time for her to have a new name."

Paige shrugged. "Okay," she said. But she didn't sound as though anything was quite "okay."

Sarah waited for more, but Paige was bent over the doll intently, and she said nothing further. After a brief moment Sarah offered, a bit too brightly, "I think Collette's a queen. Don't you?

She could be the queen of Latvinia, and we could be her subjects."

"Latvia," Paige corrected.

Sarah could feel the heat rising to her face. She had meant to say Latvia. She didn't know where that other word, *Latvinia,* had come from. But she didn't know why Paige had to make such a big deal out of it, either.

"Latvinia," she said firmly. "This is a pretend country. A country that has a doll for its queen has to be pretend."

Instead of agreeing or objecting, Paige began unbuttoning the tiny buttons in the back of the doll's dress to examine the leather body.

"I'll be the prime minister of *Latvinia"*—Sarah continued—"and you—"

"You know one of the things Valerie always does?" Paige interrupted.

"No," Sarah replied, still trying to be nice, though she was feeling less nice by the moment. "What's one of the things Valerie does?"

"She always has to be the boss of everything and everybody. At the beach, she decides when we go in swimming, when we lie in the sun, when we play a game, when we go home. If we go to get ice cream cones, she picks the flavor everyone has to order. She says that's what it means to be a DDC, that we do everything together, everything alike. Like her."

Sarah snorted. "Valerie Miller is so bossy. I've never seen anybody who likes to boss other people the way Valerie does. I'll bet she even bosses her own mother!"

A smile quirked the corners of Paige's mouth. "You can believe it. When we run out of soda, she tells her mother to go to the store to buy more. I mean, she just says, 'The Coke's gone. You've got to go get us some more.' And her mother goes!"

Sarah laughed, and Paige joined in. When the laughter faded away, Sarah waited a moment to see if Paige wanted to say anything more about Valerie and the DDCs. She wouldn't mind if she did. But Paige just sat there, fiddling with the doll's dress.

"Okay, then," Sarah said. "Collette is the queen of Latvinia. And I'll be the prime minister and you'll—"

"No!" Paige said it sharply.

Sarah straightened, surprised. "No, what? You don't even know what I was going to say."

"I'll not be whatever it is you've decided for me to be. And she's not a queen. And her name's not Collette. It's Nancy. Miss B named her *Nancy*."

"But—but—you can just look at her and see she's not a Nancy!" What had happened to Paige?

"It's no wonder," Paige said. She began buttoning the dress again.

"No wonder what?" Sarah asked, utterly confused. What were they talking about?

"It's no wonder you don't like Valerie and she doesn't like you."

The words stung. Of course Sarah knew Valerie Miller didn't like her. She'd always known. But still Paige didn't need to go and announce it that way. It sounded so . . . well, like maybe Valerie had a good reason. "Why is it no wonder?"

Instead of answering, Paige started on something else. "I never meant to join the DDCs, you know. Valerie had called me the night before. She'd promised me a cake and a movie, all kinds of things, but I wasn't going to do it."

"Then why did you? We had talked about it all. We had agreed. And then you went and let her pull you in like a fish on a line." Sarah had almost forgotten how angry she had been at Paige's betrayal. "That was really dumb."

"Because . . ." Paige paused, her hands wrapped so tightly around the doll's waist that her knuckles looked pearly. Sarah didn't think she was going to say anything more. Just because. But then Paige thrust her chin forward and continued. "Because you're so bossy. Because you had to go and answer for me."

Sarah reeled at the unfairness of the accusation. "All I said was . . ." What had she said exactly? She couldn't remember. "All I said was what we'd agreed."

"All you said was what you'd picked for me to say. You don't think I'm smart enough to answer for myself, so you made up the words and then even went and said them for me."

Sarah opened her mouth to speak, but nothing came out. Nothing at all.

Paige stood up from the bed, the doll still in her hands. "So I figured, what's the difference? You tell me what to do, what to say, or Valerie does. I decided I might as well try Valerie."

"And?"

A small smile played around Paige's mouth. "I've decided I don't need Valerie, either. That's why I left the DDCs."

"You left the DDCs?" Hope bloomed in Sarah's chest. Paige wasn't a part of Valerie's club any longer!

"Kate and I, we walked out. And we're not going back. We decided we weren't going to be bossed anymore. Not by Valerie. Not by anybody."

"You didn't tell me."

"We decided not to."

"What?" Sarah's heart clattered against her rib cage. Her mouth went suddenly dry. "Why did you and Kate *decide* not to tell me?"

"'From the frying pan into the fire.' That's what we said. Coming back to you would be almost like going from the frying pan into the fire." It was an expression Paige had learned from Miss B. It meant going from one bad thing to something worse.

"Because I'm worse than . . . Valerie?" Sarah could barely say it.

Paige considered that. "Not worse than, but you want everything your way, too. Just like her."

"And so—you—you don't—like me?" The words stumbled off Sarah's tongue.

"I don't know." Paige's eyes were serious, even sad. "I know I don't like being bossed. That's all. Except for that, I don't know."

Sarah couldn't breathe. She rose from the bed. Paige Picotte was a traitor. A traitor! Not only had she left her for the DDCs, but after all their years of being friends, all the times hidden inside the lilac bushes playing with dolls, visiting Miss B, palling around at the beach, at school, Paige didn't even like her! And here she stood, in the middle of Sarah's room, saying these terrible things and holding Sarah's doll!

"Give me my doll," she commanded. She reached for it, grabbing hold of an arm. She pulled.

To her surprise, Paige didn't let go.

A brief struggle followed. Sarah tugged. Paige gripped harder. And then—Sarah didn't know how it happened—Paige let go at last. Suddenly.

And Sarah's doll, Miss B's doll, was flying through the air. She hit the corner of the dresser with a sickening crack and dropped to the floor, landing facedown on the carpet with arms and legs splayed.

The room spun. Sarah steadied herself, one hand on the headboard of her bed. What had Paige just said to her? She'd forgotten, except she remembered it was terrible. Remote now, like the buzz of a fly in the corner of a room, but terrible. She stared at the doll, lying on the floor, and struggled for air.

When she had managed to pull air into her lungs at last, she had to struggle to push it out again.

She walked across the room and leaned over—slowly, so slowly—and put her hand on the doll's back. She lifted Collette . . . Nancy . . . and, with great care, turned her over in her hands.

The doll that had once belonged to Miss Berglund's mother was broken. A crack had split the serene bisque face, the lovely smile, in two.

"Look what you did," Sarah whispered fiercely, turning and holding the broken doll up as close to Paige's face as she dared. "Just look!"

Paige refused to look. She didn't answer, either. Not even to defend herself. She just walked out of the room.

CHAPTER 10

GROWING UP

Sarah ran a finger down the crack in the doll's face. The glue had held. She had left Miss Berglund's doll on a shelf in her closet all night with the head firmly pressed between two large books from her mother's bookshelf, *The Complete Works of Shakespeare* and *The Joy of Cooking*. The combination of Elmer's glue and the pressure from the books had done the job. Not that the crack couldn't be seen. It was still visible. Of more importance, a finger traced across the delicate china could detect it easily. But at least the doll's face no longer gaped open, revealing the mechanism that controlled the eyes. Looking at the rusty works inside the doll's head had made Sarah feel nauseous, almost as though she were peering inside the skull of some living creature.

Paige hadn't come back. Not to help repair the damage. Not to apologize for the terrible things she had said. And she *had* said terrible things. *From the frying pan into the fire? Just like Valerie?*

Sarah swiped at her cheeks with the back of her hand, first one, then the other, but she could no longer feel any wet. She had cried so much through the evening and the night that she must have run out of tears. Mom had tried to console her. Daddy had come in and sat on the side of her bed for a long time. But she couldn't explain. Not about the broken doll. Not about Paige. Only that she would never have another friend as long as she lived. She was certain she wouldn't. And her parents had refused to believe that.

But, of course, they didn't know.

She wished she were younger, four or five—even eight. Back when she could tell her parents everything. Back when they understood.

She didn't know when she had ever felt as alone in the world as she did this morning.

Because you're so bossy. Because you had to go and answer for me!

Was she as terrible as Paige said? Did it matter that she had only been trying to help? Apparently not. Even the doll's vivid blue eyes accused her.

She shook open the brown paper grocery sack she had brought to her room from the pantry and gently lowered the doll into it. She was going to take Nancy back and put her where she belonged. If only she were still whole. But there was nothing she could do about the crack. Maybe none of the women who came to help Miss B would ever look closely enough at the doll to see the crack. And maybe Miss Berglund would never lift the dome and touch the doll's ruined face.

But if she did, what would she think? Sarah knew she should tell her, but she couldn't. If Miss B were angry with her, too, she would have no one left. No one outside of her family. Family was wonderful, of course. Necessary. But it wasn't enough. A person had to have friends, too.

The bag would be in the way once she was inside Miss Berglund's house, but she needed it to get past her mother, to get past any prying neighbors who might be outside. Besides, she wouldn't feel right holding Nancy out in the open in front of Miss B. She had never taken advantage of Miss Berglund's blindness before, and she wasn't going to begin now. She might be an awful person the way Paige had said, but there were some things she wouldn't stoop to doing.

Sarah started down the stairs.

Her mother was at the desk in the living room,

writing checks. "Where are you going?" she asked as Sarah passed through the room, heading for the front door.

Sarah clutched the grocery bag tighter. "To Miss B's."

"I'm . . ." Her mother hesitated. She looked down at whatever bill was in front of her, and when she looked up again, Sarah was startled to see that her usually cheerful brown eyes were sad. But her mother said only, "I'm glad you have Miss B. I wish there were something I could do to help."

Sarah swallowed hard, nodded. Yes, she wished that, too.

And then she was out the door, still holding the brown sack tightly against her chest.

So now even her mother was hurt because she no longer had any friends. That must be what she was sad about. And how much worse would she feel if she knew her daughter was a thief, a vandal who took other people's most precious treasures without permission and then destroyed them?

Was this what it was like to grow up? To have to take responsibility for everything you did, for all the bad things you were? To know, not just that you made mistakes sometimes—everybody made mistakes, didn't they?—but that the person you were, deep inside, was . . . cracked? And to have to know that every day of your life?

Valerie Miller and the DDCs were so proud of

being double digits. They ought to think about never being single digits again. Not ever. They should think about how lonely a person could feel growing up.

Sarah shifted the bag to her other hand. Strange how heavy a small doll could be. She cut across the lawn to the point where a break in the lilac bushes made it easy to squeeze through to Miss B's yard.

The blossoms on the bushes were almost gone now. Even the tea-colored lace was mostly gone. Such a short time ago she had described them to Miss B as shimmery. How quickly everything could change!

Sarah stopped on Miss B's front porch. Before she went in, she had to figure how she was going to get Nancy back up to the bedroom. She looked around. Thomas Cat wasn't stretched out on the swing or lying in the sunlight that puddled on the porch floor. If he wasn't in the kitchen, either, she would use him as her excuse once more.

She opened the door and stepped inside, calling. "Miss B? It's me. Sarah."

"Come in," Miss Berglund called back, as she always did. "You're early today. Have you had your breakfast?"

Sarah hadn't. She hadn't even thought about food, but she didn't want to think about it now, either, so she replied, "Yes, I already ate."

"I'm making my famous scrambled eggs," Miss B called back.

Miss B's scrambled eggs *were* practically famous. They were famous for having everything in them short of the kitchen sink, as Miss Berglund herself described them. Sarah and Paige had been served the "famous" eggs more often than they liked to remember. They used to say that sometimes Miss Berglund herself didn't know what the ingredients were that made their way into her eggs, that many of the leftovers in her refrigerator were a mystery even to her.

The very worst was when she had put sardines and leftover eggplant in eggs. Both Sarah and Paige had had to tip their breakfast into their paper napkins, stuff the napkins into their pockets, and throw them away at home. Neither of their moms had been able to figure out why the laundry hamper had smelled so fishy that week.

Even though Sarah had told Miss B she'd already eaten, when she arrived in the kitchen she found an extra plate already out next to the stove. This morning the eggs Miss Berglund was stirring on the stove looked almost normal. Just chunks of tomato in them, onion, something green, too. Green beans?

"I've already eaten," Sarah said again, her words coming out with a sullen weight she hadn't intended.

Miss B, wearing a flowered dress this morning, took the pan from the burner and scooped half of the eggs onto the second plate anyway. Then she divided the rest between her own plate and a saucer that was probably intended for Thomas. "How are you, my dear?" she asked.

"Fine," Sarah replied. "Just fine." The lies, one after another, seemed to roll off her tongue. She didn't know when she had ever been less "fine." She shifted the grocery bag from hand to hand. "I was wondering, though. May I go look for Thomas Cat?"

"You don't have to go after him today," Miss B replied cheerfully. "The lazy old thing's being escorted down to breakfast this very minute."

What did that mean? Escorted down to breakfast? Sarah rolled the top of the grocery bag a bit more tightly, but stopped when the stiff brown paper crackled in her hands. She stood perfectly still, wondering what to do next, what to say.

She guessed she might as well sit down and try the eggs.

A footfall stopped her. It seemed to come from over her head. She looked at Miss B, but Miss B seemed unconcerned, so instead of sitting down, Sarah stepped through the doorway to the dining room. Someone was in Miss Berglund's house!

And there she was, as big as you please, Paige Picotte clumping down the stairs as though she owned the whole place. Even the upstairs. Even without Sarah's being there.

Thomas Cat lolled in her arms, purring.

When Paige looked past the armful of black-and-white cat to Sarah, she did not smile.

CHAPTER II

I KNOW!

Sarah whipped the grocery sack behind her back, though she realized, even as she did, that the gesture was futile. Paige's gaze followed the movement, and her eyes said she knew perfectly well what guilty secret the bag contained. Though she didn't, of course. She knew only half of it, that the doll in the bag was broken, not that Sarah had taken her without permission and was now trying to return her secretly.

Sarah didn't bother to speak. She just stepped back into the kitchen and settled into her usual chair.

What was Paige doing here anyway? She never came to Miss B's on her own. Miss B was Sarah's neighbor, Sarah's friend. Paige never would have met her if Sarah hadn't introduced them.

"I've got Thomas, Miss B," Paige announced, coming into the kitchen. "He was on your bed."

"Lazy old cat," Miss Berglund said for what must have been the thousandth time. "I suppose he thought I'd bring his breakfast upstairs." And she put the saucer of eggs on the floor.

The toaster popped, filling the air with the nutty fragrance of fresh toast. Vienna bread with sesame seeds. Sarah's favorite. Despite the fact that she wasn't hungry, her mouth watered.

Paige put Thomas down in front of his saucer and then sat down to the plate of eggs Miss B had put on the table. She picked up her fork and began to tease a bit of green out of the egg, pushing it to the edge of her plate. It was a pea. Sarah grasped the grocery bag more tightly and settled it into her lap.

"Are you sure you don't want something, too?" Miss B asked the air above Sarah's head, setting the plate of toast on the table.

"I'm sure," Sarah said. All she cared about was getting upstairs to return the doll. It was so unfair that Paige, who had no need to go there, had been upstairs. Now that Thomas had been brought down to the kitchen, what excuse could Sarah use to leave the room?

"You know," Miss B said, "Papa hated scrambled eggs. He liked them fried or even poached. He always said scrambled eggs were an abomination."

An abomination, Sarah thought. That was a good name for Miss B's eggs.

"'It's a good way to use up leftovers,' I used to tell him. 'And on what they pay you at that church, we can't afford to be wasteful.'"

Paige, who had been making a pile of vegetables at the edge of her plate, set her fork down suddenly and pulled her usual notepad and stub of a pencil out of her pocket.

Sarah gazed out the window. She had no interest in whatever Paige thought she was "observing" this time. Several bright goldfinches had clustered around Miss B's thistle feeder. Miss B loved hearing descriptions of the birds at her feeder. Sarah had asked her once why she kept the feeder when she couldn't see the birds who came to it, and birds, after all, don't usually sing at a feeder. She had said, "Just because I can't enjoy looking at them doesn't mean they don't need to eat."

Miss B was still talking about Papa, about what foods he'd liked, what ones he couldn't stand. He'd hated liver, which she said she'd always served every Tuesday because it was "good for him." He hadn't been able to abide "good, nutritious vegetables like brussels sprouts," which she'd made care to serve, too. From the litany she recited it sounded as though she had seldom prepared anything for her father that he had really enjoyed.

When Sarah looked down at the table, the small sheet had been torn from Paige's notebook and lay in front of her. All in capital letters Paige had written, I KNOW!

Sarah stared at the letters, her heart suddenly hammering in her throat. I KNOW!

What? she mouthed silently, pushing the slip of paper away. *What do you know?* She tried to look unconcerned, even bored, but her breath was ragged.

Paige took the paper back and wrote again, her fingers wrapped tightly around the pencil. She pushed the slip of paper back in front of Sarah.

At first Sarah refused to look at it. She didn't have to play this game. But then her eyes betrayed her and read the words of their own accord. I KNOW YOU STOLE THE DOLL.

The letters seemed to squirm on the page. *Stole?* She had never stolen anything in her life. She had borrowed Nancy. That was all. Nonetheless, her mouth had gone suddenly dry, and her hands shook as she grabbed the slip of paper and turned it over.

Snatching the pencil from where Paige had laid it down on the table, she wrote her reply on the back of the sheet. YOU DON'T KNOW ANY-THING. MISS B GAVE HER TO ME. She shoved the paper back at Paige.

Miss B, oblivious to their silent conversation, had moved on to talk about Papa's sermons, about how he was the best preacher, one of the most learned men in town, probably in all of Minnesota.

Paige tore off another sheet of paper with a zipper sound. Sarah watched Miss Berglund carefully, but she seemed to be too busy talking to notice.

NO, SHE DIDN'T, Paige wrote, still in those capital letters that felt like shouting.

Sarah was having trouble breathing. She took the paper and the pencil again. DID YOU ASK HER? she wrote, stabbing so hard at the paper that she broke the lead of the pencil in the middle of the question mark. If Paige had said something to Miss B about the doll's getting broken, Miss Berglund would have told Paige that she'd never given Nancy away. But Paige couldn't have told her. If she had, Miss B would have confronted Sarah about taking the doll when she'd first come in. Sarah had never known Miss B to be afraid to speak her mind.

Paige reached to take the slip of paper and the pencil from Sarah. I DIDN'T NEED TO ASK HER, she wrote, pressing hard to make the broken pencil work. I JUST KNOW.

Sarah, unable to think of an answer to the renewed accusation, scowled at Paige and slumped back in her chair.

Paige scowled back. Wrinkling her forehead that way made her freckles all run together into a blob. No wonder she hated her freckles. They looked dumb.

"Papa used to forget his collar all the time, those stiff round collars that clergymen wear. In the early years, they had to be washed and starched and ironed every day. And I had to check him before he left the house to make sure he'd put it on."

Paige joined Miss B's conversation as though she'd been listening all along. "It must have been awfully hard for you," she said sweetly. "You were only nine years old when you had to begin taking care of your father."

She made nine sound like practically a baby.

Miss B leaned forward, her face eager, her fork raised for emphasis. "But it wasn't. Don't you see? He was so special. So intelligent. He knew so many things I didn't know. Literature. Philosophy. Theology."

Sarah said nothing, though she didn't see how Papa's being intelligent would make washing and starching and ironing his clerical collars any easier. Anyway, let Paige sit there pretending to be the polite guest. Paige, who accused people of stealing.

"But still he needed me," Miss B went on. "The man couldn't iron a shirt without burning it, or himself. Or fry an egg. And if I hadn't protected him, the good ladies of the church would have eaten him up."

Sarah half smiled at the image of the church women gathered around a table with roasted pastor as the main course. But then she stopped. What did she have to smile about? She had just been accused of stealing.

By her former best friend.

That wasn't what she had done, was it? When she'd taken Miss B's doll, she had always intended to bring it back. Just as soon as she had shown it to Paige. If it hadn't been for the accident—and the accident was as much Paige's fault as hers— Miss B never would have had a clue that the doll had ever left her safe place beneath the glass dome. And even now, she would never know exactly what had happened. Why, she had no idea, even, that Sarah had been upstairs.

Sarah ran that thought by again. She didn't know I was upstairs. And again. Miss B didn't know! But Miss Berglund was aware that Paige had gone up there. Paige had just announced she'd found Thomas Cat on her bed.

An answer to all this mess was sliding, stealthily, into Sarah's brain. An answer so good—and so *mean*—that she could feel her face stretch into a smile. Didn't Paige deserve a little meanness?

Sarah reached past Paige's arm and took the pad and pencil again. She turned the pencil so as to find a bit of lead that was still exposed and formed the letters on the pad carefully. HERE, she wrote. YOU PUT NANCY BACK. IF YOU DON'T, MISS B WILL THINK YOU'RE THE ONE WHO TOOK HER. SHE DOESN'T KNOW I EVER WENT UPSTAIRS, BUT SHE <u>KNOWS</u> YOU WERE THERE.

Then, without even taking her leave of Miss Berglund, she stood, laid the grocery sack containing the broken doll on the table, put the note down in front of Paige, and left.

CHAPTER 12

FOR YOU

Sarah walked slowly down Miss B's front walk and back toward her own house. She had to walk slowly. Her knees had turned to jelly. If she tried to move fast, she would end up a lump in the middle of the sidewalk.

What had she done? What stupid thing had she done?

All Paige needed to do now was to hand the doll to Miss B and tell her the whole story. And Miss Berglund would believe her, of course. Why shouldn't she? Everyone knew Paige didn't lie.

How had Paige known that she had taken the doll without permission anyway? It wasn't as though they were still friends, as though Paige would be able, even now, to read her mind and heart the way she'd once been able to do.

Sarah reached the front stairs of her own house and sank down onto the middle step. If she waited here, she would know what Paige had done. At least she would know whether or not Paige brought the doll with her when she came out of Miss B's house.

Was it all her fault, this awful thing that had happened between them? So she had spoken up to dumb Valerie, had said what they'd both *agreed* Paige was supposed to say. But if Paige hadn't stood there like her mouth was full of mud, she wouldn't have said a word. Truly. She wouldn't have needed to.

Maybe Paige had set the whole thing up. Why else had she waited so long to answer Valerie? She'd known Sarah wouldn't be able to stand it if she didn't say anything, that sooner or later Sarah would have to speak. And then she'd have a perfectly good excuse to be angry. To be angry and to go over to the DDCs. It's probably what she'd wanted all along.

Sarah propped her elbows on her knees, cupped her chin in her hands, and stared out at the summer day. A swift, banging thunderstorm had come through during the night, leaving the morning sidewalk scribbled with worms. *Scribbled with worms.* That would have been a good eye bouquet to take to Miss B. She should have thought of it sooner.

A barely perceptible sound, a click and a *whoosh,* and the front door opened over at Miss Berglund's house. Sarah caught her breath. So soon? Was Paige coming so soon? Surely she hadn't been there long enough to have had time to go upstairs and put the doll back under the dome. She hadn't had time to give Nancy back to Miss B and explain the whole story, either.

But there she was, coming out the front door, crossing the porch—the grocery bag, held by its rolled top, in her hands.

Sarah sat perfectly still, not turning her head to appear to look, but watching out of the corner of her eye. When Paige got to the sidewalk that ran along in front of the houses, she would turn left, away from Sarah's house, toward her own home. But she didn't. She turned right instead. And then right again in front of Sarah's house. She came directly toward the steps where Sarah sat.

Sarah could see Paige's feet. She was wearing pink flip-flops. They must be new. She'd never had pink flip-flops before. Her feet were round and smooth, and they were freckled like the rest of her. Even her toes were round and freckled.

"Hi."

"Hi." Sarah's voice rose to an embarrassing squeak. She didn't look up, but she moved over so there was plenty of room for Paige to sit down if she wanted to. She propped her chin in her hands again.

For what seemed like a long time—years, eons—Paige stood there, saying nothing more. She held the grocery bag out in front of her like some kind of offering. Or perhaps more like an exhibit in a criminal trial. Sarah considered reaching out to take it, but her hand didn't seem to want to move.

Finally, Paige lowered herself to the opposite end of the step, about as far from Sarah as she could get without falling off onto the stickery bushes below, and settled the grocery bag on her lap.

"So you've still got Nancy," Sarah said when, at last, she could pull herself out from under the weight of the silence.

"I thought you'd named her Collette." Paige sounded calm, in charge. Her words were as smooth and hard as glass.

Sarah shrugged. "Miss B named her Nancy," she said.

More silence. Two squirrels chittered crossly in the oak tree in the front yard.

"I kind of liked Collette," Paige said.

"What?" Sarah straightened. "What did you say?"

Paige flushed pink. "I always like the names you pick."

Sarah snorted, dropped her chin into her hands once more. "Sure you do." Was Paige making fun of her?

For a while Paige was silent, then finally she said, speaking slowly as though the words caused her pain, "It's just that . . . I think and think and finally decide on a name, and then in two seconds you come up with something better. Sometimes it makes me kind of mad, you know?"

"I'm sorry," Sarah said. And she was. She was sorry she had ever said or done anything to make Paige feel bad. She *was* better with names—and words—than Paige, but what did that matter? Paige was a better swimmer than she was. She was better at math, and Sarah's father wanted very badly for his daughter to be good at math. Paige was better at Nintendo, too.

"You don't need to be sorry." Paige said it softly. She said it as though she meant it. "It's me I get mad at."

Sarah looked at her for the first time. Really looked at her. Wasn't Paige angry anymore? She had to be angry. "But you wanted to name your dolls yourself. You said so." *You said I'm bossy!* she wanted to add, but she couldn't make herself say that.

"It's just . . . well . . . Gertrude is my grandma's name. You know?"

"Oh," Sarah said. "Oh. I didn't know."

Paige shifted the grocery sack from one hand to the other. "I should have told you. Only the thing is . . . you see . . . I like Gwendolyn better."

"You do?"

Paige turned to look directly into her face. "Wouldn't anybody?"

Then they both laughed.

Silence fell between them again, but lighter this time, almost comfortable.

"I'm sorry about Miss B's doll," Sarah said. She said it tentatively, hopefully. "I shouldn't have taken her. I should have put her back myself. I'll find a way to do it." She reached to claim the grocery sack in Paige's lap, but Paige encircled it with a protective arm.

"Why did you take her?" she asked.

Why did I take her? Sarah tumbled back, back in her mind, trying to remember. Why had she taken Miss B's doll? Taking her *was* stealing, and she didn't steal. And stealing from a friend, especially a friend who was blind, must be the worst crime of all.

Then she remembered. "I took her for you," she said.

"For me?"

"Not to give her to you exactly. I always meant to put her back under the glass dome in Miss B's bedroom real soon. But I knew you'd love her, and

I wanted to have something you'd be willing to come to my house to see."

"Oh." Paige leaned past the sack in her lap to pick up a long twig. She used it to lift a sodden worm from the walk and return it to the grass.

Sarah watched the place in the grass where the worm had disappeared. Was it glad for the rescue or did it feel interfered with? "Do you think worms get washed out onto the sidewalks in the rain," she asked, "or do they come there on their own to get away from the wet?"

"It wouldn't have worked, you know," Paige replied, as though that were an answer to Sarah's question.

"What? What wouldn't have worked?"

"Making Miss B think I was the one who'd taken her doll."

Sarah's breath quickened. So they were back in this place again. She'd thought they were being friendly. "Why wouldn't it have worked?"

"The glue." Paige stood as she spoke, the bag still held in front of her. "When she felt the crack she would have been able to tell that her doll was broken and then glued. She would have known it was you. If I'd taken Nancy when I was upstairs today, I wouldn't have had time to break her and glue her together and then put her back again."

Sarah rose, too. She stood there nodding

stupidly. Of course Paige was right. Miss B would have known. "It was a dumb idea," she said. And then she added, giggling just a bit, "Maybe she'll think it was Papa who broke her doll."

"Maybe," Paige said, but she didn't smile.

Sarah reached for the bag again.

"So you aren't going to tell her?" Paige asked, stepping back so that the bag was just out of reach.

Sarah shrugged. "How can I? She'd hate me. She'd probably hate me forever. Nancy means a lot to her."

Paige shrugged, too, and after another long moment when neither of them spoke, she handed over the sack and turned away.

When Sarah took the grocery bag, its lightness was so astounding that her hand, prepared for the doll's weight, jerked upward, almost sending the sack flying. She tore the top open. There was nothing inside at all!

"Where is she?" Sarah cried to Paige's retreating back. "What did you do with the doll?"

Paige kept moving. She answered without turning back to face Sarah again. "She's in the chair," she called. "The one you always sit in at Miss B's kitchen table. I left her there."

CHAPTER 13

"BLAST IT, PAPA"

Sarah knelt at her bedroom window, looking down on Miss Berglund's backyard. She had been up here waiting since she had finished dinner, watching the sun flatten as it dipped toward the horizon, measuring the progress of the darkening shadows that stretched across the grass.

At last. There it was, at last! A brief flame, then the pinpoint of orange light. That's what she had been waiting for. Miss Berglund had come outside to smoke a cigarette. It was something she did every evening, even in the cold of winter, smoke the one cigarette she allowed herself each day out on the brick patio in back of the house.

And one cigarette would give Sarah just enough

time to find the doll and put her back where she belonged without being caught.

She could tell from the distant murmur of the television set that her parents were in the den watching the news, so she hurried down the stairs and out the front door, careful not to make a sound that might catch their attention.

Miss B's door opened with its usual click and sigh, and then Sarah was in the dim front room, the dining room, the kitchen. There were no lights on in the house, of course. Lights did Miss B no good. If the day was dark, Sarah and Paige always turned lights on when they came in, turned them off when they left. Sarah could have turned one on now, but she didn't. When she got to the kitchen she could see the shape of the table clearly enough anyway. The chair usually reserved for her stood directly in front of her.

Bending over the back of the chair, Sarah could make out the gleam of the doll's china hands, the pale curve of her cheeks. She let out a breath she hadn't even known she'd been holding. Clearly Miss B hadn't discovered Nancy. Sarah picked the doll up, cradling her in one arm, and headed for the stairs. It would take only a moment to put her back under the glass dome, only another to be out of the house again. And then it would all be over.

Well, almost over. There would still be the wait-ing, the wondering when Miss B would notice, what she would think when she did. There would still be the waiting and wondering, too, about Paige. Was she angry with her still? Were they friends again? What had their conversation on the front steps meant? Paige had gone home without saying a word about their seeing each other again.

Darkness lay heavily on the stairway, but moonlight sifted through Miss B's bedroom windows, making the table on the other side of the bed clearly visible. Sarah quickly found her way to it, lifted the glass dome, and settled Nancy back into the stand. Then she kissed the doll's cool bisque cheek and replaced the dome. Done! Nancy was home, as good as new. Or as close to new as anyone could make her.

Sarah hurried out of the bedroom.

She was halfway down the stairs when she heard a small sound. It was the back door opening and closing, footsteps approaching from the kitchen.

If she had reacted when she first heard the door, if she had, in that instant, scurried down the rest of the stairs not caring how much noise she made and run for the front door, she could have gotten away. Easily. She would have been off the porch and on the other side of the lilacs before Miss Berglund could have called out to ask who was there. And Miss B would never have known her friend Sarah was the one to betray her. Never!

But Sarah didn't scurry. She didn't do anything, in fact. Only stood there, frozen in the middle of the stairs, as though she had been the one imprisoned beneath glass. And the next thing she knew, Miss B was below her, a dark form beneath a cloud of white hair, slowly and steadily climbing the stairs.

Sarah backed up the steps. She kept moving, one careful, silent step at a time, until she had reached the landing. Then she continued backing down the hall, keeping the steadily approaching figure in her sight. At the end of the hall, she stopped, her back pressed against a closed door.

Miss Berglund had nearly reached the top of the stairs. She would turn right and go into her own room. Sarah was sure of that. Or as sure as she could be about a routine she had never witnessed before. She reached to grasp the doorknob pressing against her spine, turned it, and slipped into the empty room. Then she closed the door again, holding the handle tightly as it turned so the latch didn't even click, and leaned against it.

She stayed that way for a long time, waiting for her heart to quit pounding.

After a few minutes had passed with no approaching footsteps, no hand on the opposite side of the door, turning the handle, Sarah straightened and looked around. She was in Pastor Berglund's bedroom. This had to have been his, because she remembered that his bedroom was at the back of the house. Right above where Miss Berglund had her nightly cigarette.

Sarah could see little except for darkened lumps that suggested a bed, a couple of dressers, a chair. It seemed to be a perfectly ordinary bedroom, even if it had once belonged to "himself."

Sarah's hand searched out the wall switch. A little light might help her think more clearly. Though the truth was there wasn't much to think about. What choice did she have now except to wait for Miss Berglund to go to sleep and then slip down the stairs and out of her house? She took a deep breath and flipped the switch anyway.

The room that leaped before her into the light was an ordinary bedroom, as it had appeared to be in the dark. A heavy, walnut bed, a bedside table, two dressers. A leather reading chair with a floor lamp next to it. The surfaces of the dressers and table were clear except for a photo in a wooden frame on the table. Sarah moved closer and picked the photo up.

The photo was a close-up snapshot of a girl in a white dress. Who else but a young Miss B? Miss Berglund—though no one would have called her that then; her given name was Imogene, they would have called her Imogene—stood rigidly in front of some kind of greenery. The lilac bushes, maybe. Could the lilac bushes be as old as Miss

Berglund? Her chin was thrust forward, her back held very straight, her arm wrapped firmly around a doll. Collette. No, Nancy. The arm seemed to be clutching Nancy so tightly that Sarah almost expected the doll's face to show pain. But the pain she saw was entirely in the face of the girl, in her dark eyes.

Sarah didn't know when she had ever seen such sad-looking eyes. Maybe in pictures of children in refugee camps. Their eyes held the same blank despair. But the ones in the photo showed something more. They weren't just sad; they were mad, but in a way that was meant not to show.

Whoever was taking the photo was being studied, measured, and found seriously wanting.

Pastor Berglund?

But Miss B adored her father. She talked about him all the time. She even talked *to* him, didn't she?

Sarah shook her head. She must be wrong. Or else the photo had been taken by someone else.

She set the picture down on the table again. If she stayed too long, her parents would go to bed, too, and they would stop by her room to check on her when they did. Then she would be in a whole different kind of trouble.

She would open the bedroom door, nothing more. Just enough to listen for any sound of movement. If all was quiet, she could be down the stairs and out the front door in an instant. But as she started across the room, her toe caught on the braided rug next to the bed. She lurched forward, grabbing at the nearby floor lamp to stop her fall. Instead of steadying her, the lamp toppled ahead of her, hitting the hardwood floor with a resounding clatter and bang.

At first Sarah knelt there, where she had fallen, waiting. She wasn't hurt. Miraculously, the lamp didn't seem to be damaged, either. But that was, no doubt, going to be the end of her miracles, because even if Miss Berglund had already gotten into bed and gone to sleep—which seemed unlikely in so little time—no one could have stayed asleep through the amount of racket she and the lamp had just managed to make.

And then she heard it. Footsteps approaching. Steady, even quick, though Miss Berglund rarely did anything fast.

"What happened?" Miss B called. Her voice sounded wavery, old. "What's wrong?"

Sarah made no reply. She just scrambled to her feet, her gaze fastened on the door. The instant Miss B opened it, she would rush past her and out. It was her only hope.

"Blast it, Papa!" The door swung open abruptly, banging into the nearby dresser. "Will you never let me sleep?" Miss Berglund stood in the doorway, her head up, her nostrils flared as though she were trying to sniff out what she couldn't see.

Sarah didn't move. Was it possible that Miss Berglund really thought her father had made all that noise? That her dead father had knocked over the lamp? Sarah shivered and began to edge toward the door and her escape.

"Papa?" Miss B repeated. The name was a question this time. And then more faintly, "Papa?" Her trembling hands clutched a faded pink chenille robe closed just below her throat.

Sarah stopped just a few feet from the door, holding her breath.

Slowly, slowly, Miss Berglund lifted her hands to her face. She might have been a little girl hiding her eyes for a game of hide-and-seek. A moment later, when her arms fell to her sides again, her face had changed. She no longer looked frightened and angry, only sad. "You are a foolish old woman," she said, speaking so softly that Sarah had to strain to hear. "Foolish, foolish. Somebody ought to come and put you away."

To Sarah's surprise and deep dismay, Miss B tottered into the room, lowered herself slowly to the side of the bed, and began to weep.

Sarah could have slipped out of the room easily. The doorway was clear now, and even if she hadn't managed to remain completely silent,

Miss B probably wouldn't have heard anything over the sound of her own sobs. Sarah could be home free.

But again her feet seemed to be glued to the floor. She stood gazing at her elderly friend, the one who liked nothing better than to talk about what a fine man her father had been, the one who had burst into the room crying, "Blast it, Papa!" And her heart seemed to tremble.

She reached out a hand to touch Miss B's shoulder, but then drew it back, not wanting to startle her.

"Please, Miss B," she said instead, speaking very softly. "Don't cry. It's only me . . . Sarah."

CHAPTER 14

HARD WORK

"Now, my friend . . ." Miss Berglund set a mug of hot chocolate and a plate of buttered toast, cut into strips for dipping, in front of Sarah. "Tell me what you're doing knocking lamps over in my house in the middle of the night."

"It's not the middle of the night," Sarah protested, but still, she told her. All of it. About taking Nancy to lure Paige back. About renaming her Collette. Breaking her in the struggle with Paige and gluing her together again. Trying to trick Paige into being the one to put her back upstairs. She even told her about the odd talk the two of them had on the front steps.

"She hates me," she concluded.

Sarah knew, of course, that Miss Berglund would contradict her. That was what adults always did, wasn't it? Tell you how nothing was ever as bad as you thought it was.

"Paige hates you?" Miss B was sitting at the other end of the table. Neither she nor Sarah had turned on the kitchen light, but sat in the dim, watery light the moon spread across the oak table.

"I know she does," Sarah insisted, urging Miss Berglund on. Sarah knew she wouldn't believe the words when Miss B said them—*Of course not!* Miss B would say. *Paige would never hate you!*— but she wanted to hear them anyway.

But Miss Berglund, as usual, wasn't going to be like other adults. Instead of reassuring Sarah, contradicting her, she simply nodded. "I guess there's always a bit of hate in every kind of love," she said.

The words passed through Sarah like a knife. Then Paige did hate her. Miss B had just affirmed that she was right. Her best friend in all the world hated her!

Before Sarah even knew what she was going to say, she snapped back, "Like you and Papa? Like the hate in the way you *love* Papa?"

As she spoke, she remembered something she had heard her mother say once about Miss Berglund. How she had taken up smoking late in life when her father was bedridden and she was nursing him around the clock. How even though he hated cigarettes, she sat every evening under his open window and smoked. "She might as well have sat beside his bed," Mom had said, "and blown the smoke in his face."

Miss B didn't answer. Why should she? Sarah knew her question had been inexcusably rude. But Miss Berglund merely picked up a strip of buttery toast, dipped it into her mug of cocoa, and ate the soggy end off slowly. At last, she nodded again. "Yes," she agreed. "Like the hate in the way I loved Papa."

Sarah thought of the photo she had just seen, of the anger that lay deep in those dark eyes. Did Paige hate her like that? She didn't want to believe it.

"I had a chance to leave my father's house once," Miss B went on to say, as though she weren't changing the subject. "A man wanted to marry me. A kind and good man. But I turned him down."

"Because your father wouldn't let you go. Right?"

"No, he liked the young man. He wanted me to marry him."

"Then why?" Sarah shook her head as though to shake away a fog. Nothing made sense anymore.

"It's hard to remember now," Miss B answered. "Mostly I guess because my eyes were already failing. I couldn't bear the thought of learning another house, another man's foibles. I guess I couldn't bear to leave Papa, either."

"But he needed you. You've always told us how much he needed you."

In the thin moonlight, Sarah could just make out Miss Berglund's smile. "There were half a dozen ladies from the church who would have been here the instant I left. He'd have had to beat them off with a stick."

Sarah couldn't help but smile, too, at the thought of the grand old man whose portrait hung in the front room beating off church ladies with a stick.

"We were two of a kind, I guess," Miss Berglund went on. "Papa didn't much like change, either. It's why he bought this house from the church before he retired, so he could stay here—so I could stay here where I knew every cranny. I used to tell him he should have gotten a little place in Florida, maybe something in pink stucco, but he'd just say that he couldn't abide hot weather."

Sarah set down her mug of hot chocolate, let her hands fall limp in her lap. "Still . . . you hated him," she reminded Miss B, though more gently this time.

"Yes," Miss B agreed. "Hated and loved all mixed up together. But, you know, Sarah, when the love is real, it wins out in the end. Just the way it will with you and Paige."

Just the way it will with you and Paige! Sarah let the words sift through her, slowly. But did she believe them?

Then Miss B dipped another strip of toast into her cocoa and changed the subject. "Would you go get Collette for me? I haven't held her for a long time."

Sarah drew in her breath. Now she would have to face it. "You named her Nancy," she said.

"I like Collette," Miss B replied with the tiniest of shrugs.

Sarah went upstairs to get the doll, lifted her once more from beneath the glass dome, and brought her to Miss Berglund. Miss B held Nancy/Collette in her gnarled hands, ran her gentle fingers over the doll's arms and legs, smoothed the elegant dress and the soft hair. Last, she touched the crack in her face. She ran one finger the length of it several times, then settled the doll on the table in front of her.

Sarah waited.

"Well then," Miss B said. "I guess we'll both have to make do with that."

"Make do with what?" Sarah asked, her voice trembling.

"With knowing the crack is there. With knowing it's fixed as best as can be, but that it's still there."

"Isn't there something more I can do?" Sarah pleaded. "Something that will make it better?"

"No," Miss B replied flatly. "That's what you're going to have to live with. You and Paige both. That it happened and you can't make it go away."

Sarah wasn't certain whether Miss B was talking about the crack in the doll's face or the break in her and Paige's friendship. Both maybe. But she had to be able to make things right somehow. She spoke urgently. "I could come over here every day. I could read to you. Wash your dishes. Anything you wanted me to do."

"And how would that fix Collette?" Miss B asked. Her voice was soft, but there was an edge beneath the quiet words. Then Miss B patted the doll's hair and added more gently, "I was nine years old—your age exactly—when Mama gave Nancy to me. And I think she knew this doll would be the last scrap of childhood I'd have, that I'd be lost and alone and wouldn't be able to resist Papa's needing."

Sarah's head spun. Papa needed Miss B and didn't need her. Miss B loved Papa and hated him. She and Paige . . . Sarah shoved her chair back and stood abruptly. For a moment she teetered, as though the very floor beneath her feet were tipping, and had to reach down to grip the edge of the table. "Can't anything . . . anything in the entire world just be what it is?" she demanded to know. "Does growing up always have to be so hard?"

At first Sarah thought Miss B was going to go on sitting there, dipping her toast in her cooling cocoa and say nothing. But finally she lifted her face to confront Sarah with those unseeing/all-seeing eyes and replied, "I'm afraid it does, my dear. Growing up is just plain hard work."

Sarah sighed. Again, her elderly friend had told the truth, the simple and very complicated truth. "I'd better go home," Sarah said, "before my parents start worrying."

"You will tell them?" Miss B said. It was phrased as a question, but Sarah knew it wasn't really a question at all.

She stopped in her tracks. She hadn't thought of telling her parents about any of this. But then she looked at the ruined doll now back in her friend's gently searching hands and she said, "Yes, Miss B. I'll tell them."

"Good," Miss Berglund said, nodding. "That's good!"

Is it? Sarah wondered, starting for the door. Is it really good? But whether it was or not, she knew she had to do it.

There was no way around it. The DDCs might think growing up was wonderful, but it was hard work. And a girl didn't have to wait until she was ten to begin doing it.

Chapter 15

GOLDEN SUMMER

Sarah stepped out onto her front porch. Except for a pair of chickadees, scolding their *dee-dee-dee* from the lilac bushes, the morning street was quiet. The whole town was quiet. She was up so early, she would probably have the beach all to herself if she walked in that direction.

She headed down the walk past Miss Berglund's house. She would visit later, far enough into the morning that she wouldn't risk being offered breakfast. She needed to tell Miss B what her parents had said last night when she had told them everything. It wasn't so much what they had said, though, as the way they had looked and sounded that stayed with her. They had looked and sounded disappointed. Deeply disappointed in her. What they had said was that, if Miss Berglund was still willing to have her, they wanted her to go over to help their neighbor for an hour every day through the entire summer. She would do that for Miss Berglund willingly enough, even though Miss B had already reminded her that no amount of help could bring back the perfection of her beloved doll.

Maybe she would start with cleaning out the refrigerator before she was offered scrambled eggs again.

Her sandals slapping on the concrete walk, Sarah moved through the slowly waking town until she came, at last, to the edge of the beach. She hadn't been at the beach since the last time she'd come with Paige. She kicked off her sandals and picked one up in each hand before she stepped onto the cool sand.

Sarah paused beneath the willows, surveying the empty beach. Then she moved on until she'd reached the place where the lake met the wet sand. The cold water licking her toes sent shivers along her spine. She stood there for a long time until her toes grew warm again, or at least accustomed to the cold. Then she turned and began to walk along the hard-packed sand, just beyond the reach of the gently lapping water. She loved the beach and the lake. She always had. She'd been foolish to let Valerie Miller and the DDCs keep her away.

Far down the narrow stretch of sand, two figures appeared, walking toward her. Girls. Probably about her age. At first she thought it might be Paige and Kate, but she quickly saw that it wasn't.

Both of these girls had dark hair. The sun slanting across the water glinted off their white shorts, their bare legs. Their skin against the brilliant white of the shorts was brown. The rich golden brown of caramel. That was another eye bouquet she could take to Miss B.

She could see more clearly now. The girls approaching were the twins.

When Juanita and Estelle first joined their fourth-grade class, Sarah had thought that it would be nice to know them, nice to learn about living in another country, too. But then Valerie had started her club and just being or not being in Valerie's club seemed to take up everybody's energy and attention. There had been little left over for anything or anyone else.

The twins walked side by side, their heads bent close together. Had they thought, even for a moment, that they might be invited? Had they cared?

Would they want to talk to her or to anyone else from their class now?

Maybe Estelle and Juanita and Paige and Kate and she could start a new club. One where anyone could join, anyone who wanted to be a friend. They could call it the Growing Up Club.

In their club, you wouldn't have to be a certain age. Or a certain anything, for that matter. No one would have to be like anyone else or have to do what anyone else said. They would just come together because they liked one another—liked one another most of the time anyway.

Sarah lifted a hand to wave. She tried to make the wave casual, easy, but still she found herself biting her lip as she waited to see if the girls would respond.

Estelle and Juanita turned toward each other, just for a brief second, as if asking some kind of question, then slowly, rather hesitantly, they each lifted a hand, too.

Sarah took a deep breath of the fresh morning air and increased her pace. Golden summer lay spread out before her, and she hurried to meet it.